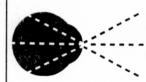

This Large Print Book carries the
Seal of Approval of N.A.V.H.

OUTLAW JUSTICE

FORD PENDLETON

WHEELER PUBLISHING

A part of Gale, Cengage Learning

GALE
CENGAGE Learning

Detroit • New York • San Francisco • New Haven, Conn • Waterville, Maine • London

GALE
CENGAGE Learning™

A portion of this novel appeared in the magazine *Thrilling Western* under the title: SONS OF THE SAGE.
Wheeler Publishing Large Print Western.
The text of this Large Print edition is unabridged.
Other aspects of the book may vary from the original edition.
Set in 16 pt. Plantin.
Printed on permanent paper.

LIBRARY OF CONGRESS CATALOGING-IN-PUBLICATION DATA

Pendleton, Ford.
  Outlaw justice / by Ford Pendleton. — Large print ed.
    p. cm. — (Wheeler Publishing large print western)
  Originally published: Hasbrouck Heights, N.J. : Graphic Pub. Co., c1954.
    ISBN-13: 978-1-4104-1839-5 (pbk. : alk. paper)
    ISBN-10: 1-4104-1839-1 (pbk. : alk. paper)
    1. Large type books. I. Title.
  PS3553.H38O94 2009
  813'.54—dc22   2009015931

Published in 2009 by arrangement with Golden West Literary Agency.

Printed in the United States of America
1 2 3 4 5 6 7 13 12 11 10 09

OUTLAW JUSTICE

ONE

Ute did all the stalling he could before he crossed Starbow's main street toward the bank's front door. It looked like the gate to perdition to him, that door. If he succeeded in doing what he meant to do inside, he would be putting an end to all he had known here in Horseshoe Basin.

He had made up his mind to it the night before. Yet once in Starbow he had found himself dreading the move far more than he had expected he would. So he had got his hair cut, had had a couple of drinks in the Rialto saloon, and he had even looked at a new saddle in the harness shop. All the while Chance Donner's bank had loomed larger in his mind than the rimrock that ran behind the town.

Still on the bank steps, he paused to touch a match to the cigarette pinched between his grim lips. He looked up the street, not seeing it but thinking of Tap Taplin. Wondering, as he had a thousand times, whether old Tap had been a foster father or the real thing.

Ute did not know the answer to that question, nor did anyone else on the Humboldt. They had buried Tap a week ago, and that had been the end of everything for Ute Taplan. Not because of the sudden, violent death that had taken Tap from the big cattle outfit called Pick. Ute was like Tap had been in that regard, at least. A man worked hard and died quick and made no complaint about either. The blow had been in Tap's will, which had all but disowned Ute Taplan.

He took a couple of absent drags on the cigarette, flipped it into the street and went on into the bank. The place was not large and had not yet lost the staleness of paper and tobacco smells trapped there through a hot night. There were a couple of clerks at work past the grill that divided the lobby. One wore an eye-shade and black cuffs and a look of ingrained preoccupation. The other was a younger man, with a shock of reddish hair. That one held a pencil in his teeth while he shuffled through a stack of papers.

Chance Donner was in his office, on ahead of Ute and at the end of the counter that ran the length of the room. Donner seemed to have noticed him hesitating outside. He was a wide-shouldered man who owned not only this institution but most of the town, while holding a great deal of the paper on the cattle outfits in the Horseshoe. He had no family. This bank was the whole of his life.

Donner did not know what was coming now. He would expect a quarrel over the way things had been left at Pick. It was no secret that the banker had taken a part in preparing Tap's will. Tap's learning had been the rustic kind growing out of a long and hard experience. Legal and financial matters were things he had always taken to Donner, and he had usually followed the man's advice.

Now Donner's rocky red face tightened as Ute strode through the door into his private room. Donner said, "Howdy, Ute. So you come in to pick a bone." He was like that, blunt, fearless and without mercy. His eyes even showed a wispy amusement for he felt that his quick challenge had taken the wind out of Ute's sails.

Ute only grinned, saying, "You can start breathing, Chance. I'm not kicking about a thing. There's no question that you made the medicine for Tap when it came to drawing up that will. But he swallowed it. He was sane of mind and sound of wind when he did. It's fine with me."

"Why," Donner said, surprised and relieved, "that's fine, Ute. I looked for you to resent Loren's getting the run of Pick. You and him compete with each other. I had a feeling that you'd lose pretty hard."

"There's only one thing," Ute said. "I wish Tap had taken the trouble to explain what he was doing. Leaving it in cold writing — well, it sounded like he was booting me out."

"He would of explained it, probably, if he hadn't been killed," Donner answered reassuringly. "And it would have been easier on you, sure. But I know what was on his mind, and I'll tell you, Ute. Loren's got a business head and he's steady. You're not only a wild one but you let your sympathy get the upper hand. Running Pick's a tough job. Tap had that to think about. He worked it out the best he knew how. Your brother's got the management, but you come in for a full half interest in the ranch and half the profit it makes. So you're not hurt anywhere, except in your pride."

Donner sounded as if that didn't amount to much. As long as a man had means, he need not worry about holding up his head.

"Glad to hear Tap thought it out for himself," Ute said narrowly. "I wasn't sure,

Chance. You lean toward Loren and never did like me. Don't get mealy-mouthed about it, either. I know you never figured me to be Tap's real son. You or somebody or something got him doubtful, and that's why he made a special will."

Donner's neck was growing red under such straight talk. He was used to having others do the listening, and he shifted uneasily in his seat. He said, "I never heard Tap express himself on what he really thought about that, Ute. The Paiutes raised you, and the point is that you kept on acting more like a wild Indian than a Taplan."

"I see," Ute said. "He figured it would be a good idea to make me a ward of Loren's. The way the Indians are of the government."

"Maybe. And Tap knew you and Loren would never make it trying to run Pick on a partnership basis. You never could get along. If that was the case while he was here, what would it be like without him around to keep you untangled?"

"Me and Loren don't get along," Ute agreed. "And it's not in me to work for him, either. So I'm pulling out."

Donner came forward in his chair, his features stiffening. He stared at Ute in sudden intentness, then said, "You drunk or

11

plain crazy?"

"Plain Injun," Ute said. "And in dead earnest. I aim to set up for myself. All I want from you is a bank loan to do it."

"Where do you aim to go, Ute?"

"Not far. I don't want to leave the Horseshoe. If you'll give me a deal I can swing, I'd like to buy the old Arbuckle place."

The banker laughed, although the surprise had not left his face. He said, "If that's your idea of how to start up in business, Tap was right about your judgment." But, foolish as the proposition had sounded to him, interest flickered in his eyes. The bank owned the old Rocking A, had taken it in on a mortgage more than once. The spread had been a white elephant as far back as Ute could recall.

"As a ward of Loren Taplan's," Ute said, "I'm not what you'd call flush. What kind of a deal can you make that doesn't call for cash? You can protect yourself by tying up my share in Pick any way you want. How about it?"

"Why, I guess something could be worked out," Donner said, and suddenly he looked relieved.

So when Ute Taplan walked out of the bank, he had changed the course of his life with one stroke of a pen. Donner had worked out a deal, all right. He had been as grasping as the law allowed, but he had also been as fair as it required. That was the measure of Chance Donner. Ethics, as far as he ever considered them at all, were what would stand up in a court of law.

And Ute had bought himself an old, hardscrabble cattle ranch that already had broken three or four owners and scared off others who had come to look it over. He had paid more than its actual value, Donner had seen to that. But Ute figured that a thing was worth what it represented to a man. By that rule, the sorry old spread was worth far more than he would be out.

For he could not tolerate the thought of keeping on at Pick. There was more involved than the hurt of Tap's post-humously divulged doubt and distrust. Ute knew that he and Loren were plain poison to each other. Better to make the break now and live apart.

Ute was about to swing aboard his horse when Ginny Ide came out of Trowe's Mercantile, across the sidewalk from him. He heard his name and looked up, and she was smiling at him, her arms full of bundles. She was a pretty girl, trim, dark and small. Her nose was tip-tilted, her eyes wide apart.

Her mouth looked warm and felt it, too. Ute knew. He had kissed it more than once.

"I thought Pick was getting set for round-up," Ginny said. "What are you doing off here in town?"

"Cutting my own throat, maybe," Ute said. "And the question goes for you, too. Aren't you going with the wagon this year?"

"I aim to try."

Ginny looked pleased at his wondering, and Ute could see that she figured on them riding home together now. She had been after him for a long while, making some headway, too. That had Ute a little leery. A man had no business to marry a girl just because it was fun to kiss her.

Looking up at him, Ginny added, "I'm in the buckboard. Why don't you tie on behind?"

"Got to go by Crosscut," Ute lied.

There wasn't a better sport in the basin than Ginny Ide. Thrown from a horse, she would get right back on. Dodged by a man, she would smile it off as she did now. Ute knew her pretty well.

"I hope I see you on round-up, then," Ginny said, and she went on up the sidewalk.

Ute watched her go, regret in him. It was a shame that so much affection was there waiting, and him not in the market for it at all. But Ginny knew all about Olivia. She had known all along how things stood with Ute Taplan.

Starbow's street looked different from what it had before he had finally gone into Donner's bank and got the thing done. The same cow ponies were strung out at the hitching rails, with the same occasional wagon or buckboard mixed in. Men in the same worn, dusty clothes still passed through the doorways on the same kind of business.

But there was a change, and he knew it to be in his own outlook. He no longer considered himself to be a part of Pick, the biggest outfit in the basin. He was hardly anything at all, not even one of the two-bit ranchers — not yet. He had a lot more to cut before he could call himself what he hoped to be, a man of dignity and independence.

He went out of town at his usual swift gait, astride a red gelding he had trained from colthood. He was a tall, lithe figure in the saddle, and after ten years in leather he still rode with something of an Indian's slack, toed-out seat.

The Horseshoe was one of the great cattle basins of northern Nevada, a wheeling vastness of hot earth blanketed by sagebrush that gave way occasionally to juniper and piñon stands. He knew it intimately. There had been long stretches in his happier days on Pick when he had forgotten all about the hot Black Rock desert. That was a region over west where roamed the Paiutes who had reared him from babyhood to the age of thirteen.

Herb Latamore was home on Crosscut, when Ute reached there — and, of more importance, so was Olivia. Ute pulled up in the ranchyard, seeing a neat, prosperous-looking clutter of buildings. But his gaze slid from these to the chestnut-haired girl it sought so eagerly. She was on the porch of the big house. It was late in the afternoon but not yet quitting time, so Ute had neither expected nor wanted to see her father there with her. He stopped at the steps and swung out of the leather.

"Howdy, Ute," Herb called from his rocking chair on the porch. "Been expecting somebody over from Pick. Been wondering if you'd run the wagon again this year."

"Why not, Herb?" Ute asked, surprised at such a question.

"Well," Herb said, and then he shrugged and fell silent.

He had come into the basin, Ute knew, at

about the time Tap did. They had been friends in the way that a less aggressive and successful man can be friendly with a fireball like Tap. Now Herb was not bothering to hide his knowledge, nor his dislike of the fact, that Loren was not Tap's spit and image.

The biggest outfit in a round-up district put up the chuck-wagon and furnished the grub. Smaller ranches sent men who ate free. Olivia was frowning now, but mainly because of her father's clear innuendo. She knew as well as Herb did that Loren watched nickels the way Tap — or even Ute — would have watched the dollars. She would not deny that. It was just that Herb's blunt way could sometimes embarrass her.

She had on a denim riding skirt and boots that had had plenty of wear. The thighs that showed through the well-fitting skirt were long and slim. Her lips were full, her cheekbones high, while her eyes exactly matched the dark brown of her hair. She had a private thing with Ute, a way of talking to him without words. She let the frown give way to one of her slight, intimate smiles. The sight of it put an extra thump in the beat of his heart.

He wanted to tell her privately of the deal he had made in town, and maybe she would arrange it so that he had the chance. He hoped so, for he never got her alone to himself enough.

"Loren set the round-up date yet?" Olivia asked.

He gave her a quick, sharp stare, then got on top of that. She would not try to rub it in about Loren now being the boss on Pick. He had not seen her since Tap's funeral but knew that she most likely resented the way things had been left.

"He says the first of next week," Ute told her. "Been slow getting the word around because of the funeral and everything. But it will be the same as always, Herb, as far as I know."

"Hope you're right," Herb said. Ute flashed a glance at him. The man had sounded downright uncertain.

Ute visited with them together a while, but because he wanted to tow Olivia off and thought he knew how, he soon said that he had to be going. To his surprise, she did not offer to ride a piece with him, the way she did more often than not. So Ute left, with all that he had wanted to tell her remaining unspoken.

Maybe Herb's mood had troubled her, as it had Ute. He knew what was on the man's mind. He distrusted Loren. Take any cattle country, and the big outfit could spell the difference between good and bad going for the rest, depending on its attitude and how it treated its small neighbors. The thing worked the other way, too, for a big ranch needed support from the outfits around it. Tap had always recognized that.

Leaving Crosscut, Ute struck out straight for Pick. The sun was lowering, its heat now full on his back. He still retained the sense of oneness with the earth that his childhood had given him. The scent of sage was as familiar as his own breath, while the purple-hazed mountains on all the horizons were the natural walls of home. Sometimes he would feel a distinct urge to peel off and let the disturbed air come against his bare brown skin as his horse rushed onward. And sometimes he would feel the savagery boil through him that Loren claimed was there all the time.

An hour's such riding brought him to the headland west of Pick headquarters. He paused there for a long look because he was moving out now, although he did not figure on divulging that to Loren or the crew as yet. The big house was old and rambling, strung out under a stand of cottonwood trees by the creek. The outbuildings and corrals ran helter-skelter. Tap had built his initial plant then had added to it again and again. But everything was in good shape and the spread ran like a well-oiled clock.

Familiar as all these things were, they had worn a different look in recent days. The change was felt rather than discerned by the eye. Pick's personality was gone, as far as he was concerned, buried forever with Tap. Ute rode on in to the day corral and put up his horse.

It was now after quitting time, and the crew was in from work. The punchers had always treated him as one of themselves, which was the way he had wanted it, although they had steered clear of Loren as much as they could. But there was a difference in that respect now, too. Over the years, most of them had all but forgotten that there was doubt as to Ute's really being Tap's son. That had come to the fore again in the way Tap had left things strictly in Loren's hands. The handling had made it pretty clear that he had entertained considerable doubt of it. Ute had become a half owner without any voice in anything. That fact made the punchers uneasy with him. They didn't know how to treat him any more, nor he them.

He was washing up at the bench in front of the bunkhouse when he saw Loren ride in with Joe Lake, who had been Tap's ramrod and was staying on as Loren's. They were talking as they rode past and were still at it when they came back from the corrals and went into the big house.

Loren was dark and slender, with a set of good looks that Tap had claimed threw back a long way, since all the Taplans he had ever seen were ugly. Lake was wedgy, gray, as hard-eyed as a gambler, and a first-rate cattleman.

By the time Ute had combed his hair, one of the punchers had come up to the bench to wash. He was a bandy-legged runt nobody had ever dared to cross twice. The only name he had ever divulged was Brig. Since it was suspected that he had come from Utah, a bunkhouse wit had once called him a refugee from a harem. He only made that one joke with Brig, and nobody ever tried to josh the man afterward.

Brig had a drawling way of talking and said, "Ute, you ought to take a look at that cut of yours up on Broken Back. I come down through there today."

"What's wrong, Brig?" Ute said. Broken Back was a rocky plateau over east of headquarters. Ute had been running the stocker stuff that Tap had given him, on what was reckoned to be his twenty-first birthday, up in that general region. They were the steers he meant to use as starters on the old Arbuckle spread.

"Better take your own look," Brig answered in his drawly way. The man was a queer one, blazing his own trails and touchily independent about it.

But he was possessed of common sense. Ute guessed it was something Brig figured a cowhand had better not say too much about to one of the owners.

Two

Ute ate an early supper, then saddled a fresh horse and rode out again. It was quite a ride to the Broken Back, and dusk had run in by the time he got there. At first he could not see a thing wrong. The stuff was of a breed that Tap had built up for himself, mostly Shorthorn and Hereford, with a little of the old Spanish strain still showing. That made for hardy stock, the steers being good rustlers but not breachy and hard to manage, the way some built-ups became.

Ute had settled his little cut here the previous spring and had been up a few times during the summer. It looked all right to him at first. But it was short in count. He did not realize that until he had made the best tally that he could of the scattered steers. It was not likely that Brig had made any better count of them, himself. He must have seen some sign of why it was short, which had led him to drop his hint.

And short it was, maybe to the extent of a hundred head. Astonished and deeply worried, Ute scouted around. He had been figuring on a shoestring start at the very best. He had to find out what was wrong here. But darkness soon put a stop to his investigation. He tried to argue himself out of a deepening concern, but it clung and still rode him when he got back to Pick headquarters.

Loren, he found, had sent Brig and two others off to inform the neighboring ranchers of the round-up starting date. But Ute doubted that he could have got much more out of Brig, anyhow. The man was a puzzler, a law unto himself, and no one's easy mark.

Seeing light in the ranch office, Ute crossed the ranchyard. Loren occupied Tap's old chair, sitting solidly at the desk as if he had always belonged there. He gave Ute a quick, close look and nodded. He had changed notably in the one week since Tap had been killed and buried. As far as Ute knew, Loren had had no more knowledge than himself of Tap's arrangement for Pick after his death. Donner's disclosure of those plans following the funeral seemed to have wiped away Loren's grief. He was elated, and a natural arrogance had come to take the fore in him.

"Howdy, kid," Loren said, for he had tried to stay on friendly terms. "Where have you been at this time of the day?"

"Up on Broken Back," Ute said. "Loren, I'm short a lot of steers."

"You are?" Loren said. "You sure?"

"No doubt about it."

"What got you worried?"

Ute did not want to implicate Brig. He simply shrugged, saying, "I hadn't been up there for a long while. After we start the round-up, I won't get the chance for another long time. And by the way, Loren, I told Herb Latamore that you figure to start the first of the week."

"Glad you did. But what do you think is wrong on Broken Back?"

"Looks like an open and shut case of rustling. There's nothing up there to tempt a steer to stray off very far. I'll take another look for sign in the morning." He was blamed if he would ask Loren's permission to take the time off.

Loren frowned. "I had something else I

wanted you to do. But maybe you better see what's gone wrong up there." The plain way in which he was showing his newly gained authority nettled Ute again. Every day since the change in their situation, Loren had gone out of his way to give some kind of order. Just as there had been hardly a day in all the years when he had not got over some reference to Ute's beclouded past.

Loren relished the fact that there was no doubt as to his own parenthood. He had been the first to come up with the nickname Paiute, which had worn down to its present form over the years. Ute had meant to keep the news to himself for a while, but his anger changed his mind.

He said, "And another thing, Loren. I'll help you through round-up, but right afterward I'm pulling out. I made a deal with Donner today. Bought the old Arbuckle spread."

"You what?" Loren said and came forward in his chair, his mouth opening wider. "But why?"

Ute grinned at him. "Because I'd rather be poor and independent than rich and another man's man. Especially yours."

"So you're sorer than I figured," Loren said. "Hoped for a while that you'd be broad-minded about it. You've got no reason to get your dander up at me, Ute. I never made the will. It was the same surprise to me as it was to you. If you'd let yourself cool off about it, you'd see that."

"I'm not sore," Ute retorted. "Anyhow, not the way you think. I always had hopes that some day some kind of new proof would come along about me being the kid Tap lost to the Indians. Nothing did, and it looks like he'd changed his mind about it, himself."

"He never was sure," Loren said readily. "And you've got no reason to feel hurt. You're smart enough, so you must remember what a ringtailed snorter you were when Tap first got you off the Black Rock and brought you here to live. Who wouldn't be one after living ten years with the Paiutes? The trouble was, you never really got over being an Injun. You still go wild when something riles you. Or else, when something works on your sympathy, you're like an Indian there, too. You'll give away everything you've got. That's what Tap had in his mind. He was protecting you, as much as me."

"Sure. Making a ward out of me. But why couldn't he have explained that to me, himself?"

"Did he know that he was going to be

thrown from a horse and drug to death? Any more than you and me ever figured he'd come to that kind of an end?" Then, hesitating a minute, Loren added, "How did you buy the Arbuckle place?"

"Ask Donner the next time you see him," Ute answered, and he walked out. He had a feeling that while Loren had been jolted by what he had done, he had not been entirely displeased. Loren knew that Pick was not big enough for both of them, and he certainly had his own ideas as to who should be the one to remain.

There was not much sleep for Ute that night, and what he got was uneasy. He dreamed an old haunting dream of his, the one that always took him back among the Paiutes and into the years he could still remember clearly, when he had believed himself to be one of them.

He had been around three years old when they had taken him off a wagon train of settlers, they had told Tap. A squaw whom Ute still thought of as his mother had brought him up. He had grown to what had been estimated the age of thirteen, as much a Paiute as any of his childhood playmates except for one outstanding characteristic. Although burned by the desert's pitiless sun until he was nearly as dark as they, he had

27

possessed a thatch of crisp and surly yellow hair. That was what had caused all the excitement, after the railroad came through and towns appeared on the desert.

His Indian village had visited Winnemucca, where he had attracted considerable attention because of his appearance. It had got in the papers about a yellow-haired boy living with the Indians. Up in the Humboldt, Tap had read the story about it. He had gone at once to Winnemucca and had learned enough to convince him only that the child could have been his own lost son. So Tap had given Ute the benefit of the doubt and brought him home to Pick.

Tap had come west to California with a wagon train that had been all but wiped out on the Black Rock Desert. The surviving emigrants had been compelled to crawl from the attacked train and lose themselves in the awful wastes. In that escape, Tap had taken charge of Loren, who had been seven years old. His wife had tried to fend for their baby son — a child with yellow hair. She had been killed and the infant had vanished from sight.

Later Tap had left California and moved to the Humboldt as so many were doing, to set himself up in the cattle business. He had built the great ranch that even then had been called Pick, a cowman's descriptive term for the letter T that had always been the Taplan brand. He had raised his sons as equals except, Ute now suspected, he had never given them full equality in his own heart. That was what hurt, because Ute had come to love the big, ferocious-looking man as only a stray can love someone who has taken it in.

Although he had strained at it time and again in his need to know his true past, Ute could not remember a thing about an attacked wagon train. The first real fear of his life had been when he had been torn away from his Indian family by the stern-looking white man and carried off to learn new ways and start a strange new life . . .

He rose early the next morning, not knowing what he would find on Broken Back. He got his breakfast ahead of the crew, slapped a booted saddle on his red gelding and slid his Winchester into the boot. Then he rode out, getting away before anybody but the cook and wrangler were stirring about headquarters.

Balmy though the morning was, he sat his saddle in mounting tension as he rode. The valley curved on a slow wide bend toward the east, uniting with a basin that had the shape of a giant horseshoe. North of Pick's headquarters, the grazing floor lifted into scrub timber, which gave way in time to roughs. Along that edge of the basin were many grassy benches and upland meadows such as Broken Back. The badlands always had made it a risky business to run cattle or horses in that vicinity. Because of the nature of the country, they became rustlers' bait.

When he topped onto Broken Back, Ute began a careful scout, riding the edge of the meadow. He had come half circle before he picked up any sign. It emerged all at once, copious evidence. The missing cut had been run off by a man on a long-strided horse. It had been a bold foray and nothing had been done at this point by way of concealing the sign.

Ute felt the hot bite of anger as he set out to follow a trail he knew could not have been very old. This was what Brig had seen, and it was queer that the man had not said so straight out. Cow sign ran onward, up through a rocky draw, then down across a bare plateau to the broken edge of the roughland. It led on through a rim break into a canyon, and at the end of this it broke out onto a sterile flat. Ute's every instinct was alert, and it was one of the times when he was glad of his early, savage training.

He could ride sign that baffled other white men. This stuff was like following a railroad track. He could do some guessing about it. A rustler preferred rough country in which to play a game of hide-and-seek. This one was bending his course due west, at right angles to his direction when he had entered the malpais. Presently, Ute suspected, he would shift his course left again and come back out into the open country. Then he would skedaddle. No man could foul the trail of as many cattle as were involved here. This one had depended upon a head start to help him get away with the cut.

Ute had gone down the flat and was turning back toward the low rim, as he had expected he would, when his sharp eyes caught the glint of something disturbing ahead of him. He did not know immediately what it was, but that awareness was all that saved him. A rifle cracked viciously at the top of the forward rim, in the split second in which he swung the gelding hard aside. The open flat offered no concealment, which doubtless was why the ambusher had chosen the spot. Ute swung the horse back and forth, bent down on its neck, progressing zigzag toward the rim.

He pulled up the Winchester, kicked off the safety, and straightened to fire at a spot where he had seen a puff of smoke. The other rifle answered, and this time he saw the bullet plow into the sandy soil as the gelding streaked past. The man was aiming so as to lead the target, the broken quartering of Ute's mount keeping him from finishing the job then and there.

Exposed, not daring to hope that he could reach safe cover, Ute felt only a boiling rage. For all the moment's racking intensity, he was wondering curiously why a rustler would wait this long to cover his back trail. It just did not make sense. A man with a stolen beef cut tried to get it where he could dispose of it in the shortest possible time. This thing had all the earmarks of a set, carefully baited trap.

Ute's evident rage and his resulting recklessness seemed to rattle the ambusher. He emptied his weapon in stitching the ground close to the plunging, swerving gelding. Ute counted the shots and held his breath through the short time in which the man reloaded his piece. In that interval, Ute made the rocks that ran out a distance from the bottom of the bluff.

For a moment, thereafter, he could only sit his heaving mount, too weak to move himself. Then the shaking emptiness left him, and his brow knit down in a dark frown. It was what Loren called his Paiute look, and it presaged a heedless violence.

Leaving the horse with its reins secured by a heavy rock, Ute went forward. The man up above had lost track of his quarry. Ute came in against the bluff beyond a bulge that cut him off from the other's sight. At this point it was only fifty or sixty feet on to the top of the rim. Ute had a hand gun in his holster, and now he let go of the rifle and started the hard upward climb.

The ascent was extremely difficult, but he scarcely paused as he went up, finding fissures with his fingers and toes. That also was part of his Paiute training, a residue from the savage life that had given him an almost feral competence, courage and even cruelty. He crawled over the top and pressed flat, his cheek on the hot rock. But the swell of the top concealed what he sought. When he looked up, he could see only the place where the rock broke against the depths of the sky.

He pulled the .45 then and began to crawl forward. He had not reached the crest in the rock when he heard a horse thunder out. Heedlessly then he shoved to his feet and bolted forward. This bench was typical of the immediate vicinity, an old earth fault that tilted down on its far end without a break until it reached the bottom. The man had brought his horse up for a fast escape and was bent flat on its back.

He was not a big figure in the saddle at best. With an acid wish for his rifle, now, Ute chopped down with his pistol. He shot at the horse's receding rump, his only halfway hopeful target. The shot made the horse buck, but the rider kept seat. Then horse and rider whipped down into the lower rock field and vanished from view.

Ute had not been able to see the brand nor any other distinguishing marks on the horse. But when the rider had raised up in order to stick the animal, Ute thought he had recognized him. A small man — a bantam — a man cut to the pattern of the mysterious Brig.

It did not all add up for Ute until, warily now, he had ridden the cattle sign on through. The trail broke back onto the open range before it was past Pick's west boundary line. And there, in another of Pick's upland meadows, grazed Ute's steers — the ones he had thought were lost for good. He took only the time required to make certain that they were all there. Then he headed for home.

He was sickened by what confronted him and could not be denied. There was no real rustling involved. Brig had baited him into a murder trap that had failed only by the narrowest of margins. But, had it succeeded, it would have been called rustlers' work, with plenty of sign around to support that theory.

Brig himself had no motive for murder, unless he had been hired for the job. The only one who would hire him would be Ute's joint heir to Tap's estate, Loren, who would have it all if he became the sole survivor. Loren — his supposed brother.

THREE

Even without being aroused as he was, Ute was not built to keep his peace or bide his time. The morning was still barely started when he got back to headquarters. But the punchers were already out on their day's work. He had not tried to pick up his attacker's trail but to beat him in and be on hand when Brig came back on a pinked horse or else on foot. Ute was now certain that he had hit the horse, and a wounded one was not an easy thing to dispose of ever.

Loren was not in the ranch office, and Joe Lake was off somewhere, too. Now fuming and again turned sick by his suspicions, Ute seated himself at Tap's old desk and tried to figure out his best course. Always some arresting factor arose to defeat that intention. He was too uncertain of too many things to act as yet. He thought it had been Brig, but had it been? If it had, he thought that Brig could only be acting for Loren, but was that so? He had to unearth more facts, he decided, hard as it was going to be for a man of his nature to have to watch and wait.

A haunt of Tap's as his bedroom had been, was no longer remindful of the man. The same fixtures were there, a desk that had been scuffed and rowelled into an eyesore, the squeaky swivel chair whose seat had been worn slick, the cuspidors that always seemed to rest off-target and — on the walls — calendars of every vintage retained because Tap had liked the pictures on them. But Loren seemed already to have imposed his own personality upon the office, which was a distinct profanity to Ute.

Now that he was here at the old desk, he thought of something that he wanted to do. Tap had owned a map of the Horseshoe, and Ute wanted to refresh his memory of the boundaries of his new ranch, the old Rocking A. He knew where the map had been kept and, pulling open a drawer, he got it out of the litter revealed. The map showed all the ranches in the basin, and now it displayed something more that at once puzzled him deeply.

The cattle outfits were superimposed on the map, their boundary lines carefully drawn and with ranch brands there to identify each of them. Tap had done that much for his own handy reference. But now each place was numbered in a small, precise hand. The figures were jumbled in such a way that they seemed meaningless. Ute puzzled over them for a while, then took a stubby pencil and an old envelope lying on the desk.

He copied off the ranch names, putting the figures assigned to each in their consecutive order. He did not understand it, even then, but number one ranch became Herb Latamore's Crosscut, the second one Pothook, and so on down through the basin. Only the useless Arbuckle spread had been omitted from the list. Ute pecked at that omission, wondering if it might furnish a clue to the meaning of this. Only that ignored spread was unoccupied and without value — he shook his head, not liking the continuing run of his suspicions.

He folded the list he had made and put it away in his pocket. He had got up from the desk when two horses appeared beyond the dusty windows. He felt an instant jolt of surprise, then a deepening of bewilderment.

Ginny Ide, looking like a curly-topped boy, swung out of the saddle. She had led in another horse, with Pick's big T brand on its shoulder. The horse was bloody from its near haunch to the knee, and as it halted it shot its hip to take the weight off the injured part. Ute shoved to the doorway, his mouth hanging open.

"Where did you get him, Ginny?" he greeted the girl.

She looked puzzled, and the fierceness of his voice seemed to frighten her a little. "Why, up on the plateau," she said.

"No saddle?"

She shook her head. "He was just like this when I found him. Heaving and bleeding. Soon as I saw the brand, I dabbed a loop on him and brought him down. How could he have got hurt that way, Ute? It looks to me like a bullet wound."

"It sure is," Ute agreed. "Thanks, Ginny. We'll doctor him."

He wasn't saying anything, but he knew now what had happened up there on Broken Back. Brig had picked up another horse on the range and changed the saddle to it. He had been in a panicked hurry, and the fact that he had left this animal where it was bound to be found soon told the rest of it.

Brig feared that he had been identified and was clearing out of the country.

"I'd started over to tell you that I'm going on round-up," Ginny said. "Dad's not feeling up to it. You don't suppose Loren will mind?"

He shook his head. Ross Ide had a bad case of rheumatism. Riding was always hard for him and often out of the question. Ginny was substituting for him more and more often. A woman could be a nuisance on round-up, but nobody ever minded having Ginny along. She did more than her share of the work and could hold her own with any man without losing his liking or respect.

Two horses came off the bottomland, and their riders were Loren and Joe Lake. The men moved indolently, engrossed in their interminable talk, as they came up into the ranchyard. But when they saw the bloody Pick horse, something happened.

Ute did not know just what it was. Ranch horses often got hurt, and the two men were still too far away to recognize this one as bullet-wounded. But they were where they could see the brand. The horse was without saddle and it was hurt. Neither man was quick enough in wiping the shock off his features as they rode in closer.

Ute was sure in that moment that they

knew something of what had happened on Broken Back. The same insight told him what he himself would have to do about it. He was warned, but he had to play a waiting game. He was now convinced that the writing on the basin map meant something of great importance and that it involved a lot of people.

The men rode in, touching their hats to Ginny. "What you got there?" Loren asked her.

She made an odd smile and said, "It looks like one of your horses got into a gun fight. I found this fellow on the plateau, sweated and bloody."

"Brig rode him out this morning," Ute said, not sure of that but trying a shot in the dark.

"Well, I'll be blamed," Loren said. "Joe, we'd better go see what happened to Brig. Only last night Ute said he thought he'd been rustled on."

"If a rustler knocked Brig loose from the saddle," Ute said, "he also knocked the saddle off this horse."

Lake covered that one quickly, saying, "Looks like Brig caught himself another horse. He's a tough little huckleberry. Probably took out after the skunk that gave him the trouble."

"Or else hit for the skyline," Ute said, and Lake flung him a quick, hard stare.

Without asking Ute to join them, Lake and Loren rode out again. Ginny, sensing the undercurrents that had run through the talk, was tense and impersonal suddenly. But she could divine nothing of the true situation, Ute knew. She had found him here idling and could not connect him with what had happened in the roughs. She probably had put it down to the old friction between the Taplan boys. That was basin gossip.

Then she said, "Ute, I don't like it a little bit."

"Don't like what?"

"This horse — what it means. Something's wrong. The way you sparred with Loren and Lake — well, you know more about this than you're telling. It gives me an awful feeling."

"Nothing to worry about, Ginny," he said. "It looks like there's rustling going on, all right. You can bet it won't keep on very long."

"I hope that's all it is," she said, and then she left.

He watched until the ground swell had cut her from sight. He had not known her nearly as long as he had known Olivia, for

Ross Ide had not moved into the basin until a few years back. But Ginny had shown a frank and durable interest in him right from the start, and a man found that pleasing to his pride. He had never gone after his pleasure in the way some men might have with a girl of her impulsive nature. That is, not far. A couple of times he had stolen a few kisses, but that was all.

He spent the rest of that day visiting the Rocking A, a brand which despite its hard luck history he meant to make his own. The layout was anything but inspiring. The whole section hugged Twist Creek, which was dry at this season. There was some back range that climbed the plateau, and behind that was the rough country in all its vast awesomeness.

The weedy sod contributed to the ranch's poverty, but the bankrupting factor had been a lack of water. Yet Ute thought he knew how to bring Twist Creek back, and that was the source of his determination to re-establish the spread as a going concern.

The ranch buildings, he thought, would only make sore eyes sorer. The original house had been built of chinked logs. To that a frame addition had been made, hastily and inexpertly. The addition was sagging and ready to let go, but the log part of the structure was as sound as ever.

There were shade trees, with a good well at the house and a few more scattered across the range. There was a pole barn still in fair shape and a number of pole corrals. The emptiness of the place, the litter reminding of so many occupancies, was a bald and disheartening sight to him.

Nonetheless, a sense of possession made itself felt in him. He would not change the house much, he decided, not at first. He could live in a cave if he had to — didn't Loren like to call him an Indian? But he would repair the barn and corrals right off. He would need winter feed until the range could be brought back, and he would have to get that in between round-up and the first bad weather.

He would play his cards thereafter as his hand and that of fate seemed to indicate. Certainly he was convinced now that he faced a proposition much tougher than bringing back a bankrupt cattle spread. There were hidden things, welling out of human passions, to be considered first and foremost. He knew Brig had tried to murder him, and in all probability done so on Loren's orders. He knew that Chance Donner, who had exercised so much influence over Pick's affairs, was not without his personal interest in the way he had persuaded Tap to leave things.

Maybe they both thought he was a real Indian or the get of some squaw favoring a white man in return for a hand mirror or a piece of calico for a dress. They seemed to hold against him the resentments so many white people harbored against Indians, denying their right to possess anything that the white ones wanted, setting them up as incompetents to be plucked, plundered and pushed around.

Ute was on the point of starting back to Pick when he changed his mind. It was not far from where he was to Crosscut headquarters, and he was not satisfied with the way Olivia had treated him on his last visit. He had puzzled ever since over the aloofness she had shown him and for the first time. Maybe she felt that while he was grieving for Tap she should keep in the background. Or maybe she had something in her craw that he did not realize. He decided on a side trip to Crosscut before he went home.

The day was warm, serene, with only now and then the faintest stir of breeze. He felt the rise of spirits that always came when he was in the openland. His senses were keener than most men's, he had observed, and they were drawn steadily to the roundabout by the small and secret stirrings of nature. He watched a distant coyote arouse at his coming and bound off through the sage, and he did not draw and wham a shot at it the way most stockmen would have done.

He retained that much from the Indians, a sense of kinship with the lower orders of life, a feeling that man was not as exalted in the scheme of things as he pretended. Again he saw a sage hen go scuttling off with her hatch in tow. He watched a camp robber hang in suspension above a distant crop of rock.

Crosscut had two riders, but both were off with Herb somewhere, and Olivia was alone at the house. She had not discerned Ute's horse to be foreign to the ranch, and thus he caught her in the kitchen where she was busy baking bread.

Looking out across the porch at him, she called, "Why, Ute — you scared me out of a year's growth."

"Like your present size," he said and swung down. Trailing the reins of the horse, he crossed the porch, glad that he had a chance to do some talking. He said, "I smell something better than bread."

"Spice cake. And there's coffee left. You

wait out there. It's as hot outside the oven as in, in here."

He settled himself into Herb's rocking chair with a sense of peace rising in him. He heard her move about in the kitchen, a quick, light tread, and his mind formed a pleasant picture of her. Yet when she came out to him, carrying coffee and cake, she did not quite fit the picture. She was still remote. Something was bothering her, all right. He took the cake onto his lap and accepted the coffee.

Bluntly, he said, "You've got something in your craw, Livvy. What is it?"

"Well, yes." She took seat across from him, perching herself on the bannister of the porch. "What are you going to do about it?"

"About what?"

"About what's bothering me. The fact that somebody has to tell you you've had a dirty deal. Are you going to let things stand the way they were left?"

"What could I do about it?" he asked.

"I don't know. But you could see a lawyer. Anybody besides Chance Donner, who could tell you whether that arrangement would stand up in court."

He had started to lift a bite of cake, but he put it back on the plate. He said, "If Tap wanted it like it is, I wouldn't want it

46

changed."

"It's going to be Loren or you, Ute. Even Dad thinks that. And there's hardly a man in the basin who wouldn't rather see you on Pick. The Lord knows I would. Ute, it seems to me the first thing you've got to do is try and break that will and get your full say in Pick as well as a financial interest in it. You owe it to the basin. Loren's not going to be easy on us if things stay like they are."

Ute had wanted to tell her about buying the Arbuckle spread, through that transaction having turned his back on Pick entirely. He had a disturbing wonder suddenly if she would like that move at all. He had not questioned it, previously, had taken it for granted that she would come there to live with him when he had built it into a paying proposition. Now he was less sure of that, was not sure of it at all.

He said, "Having a piece of Pick never meant much to me. It was a piece of Tap that I wanted. I never really had it, and that's clear. So I don't figure to do anything about it."

She came to a stand and was angrier than he thought she had reason to be. She said, "Sentiment's all right, Ute. But you can't ignore practical things. And there's something I ought to let you know. Loren's taken to coming over here, lately — or did you realize that?"

"I don't keep track of him."

"Well, he's dropped some hints. He doesn't expect you to stay on Pick very long."

"He knows damned well I won't," Ute blazed. "But what are you driving at, Olivia? I know he's always wanted you. Does he think that if he can knock me out of the picture he'll have you?"

"Ute," Olivia said coolly, "you've always assumed a great deal more than exists in fact. I love you, and we both know it, but I'm not sure what kind of love it is. We grew up together like a brother and sister. You were such a forlorn kid when you came here that my heart went out to you. That's what's got me riled now, I guess. Tap hurt you and had no right to do it. Loren will compound that hurt if he can. I want you to do something about it, Ute. You've got to. Do you understand me?"

He shook his head. "No, I don't. Are you any clearer on how you feel about Loren?"

"I like him, and in a different way. I respect his steadiness and competence. I hate to say this, Ute, but Tap's qualities show up in him better. He wouldn't have taken a thing like you have lying down."

"Warning me," he said darkly, "that I've got to show more fight or lose you."

"Ute, maybe I am. I don't expect you to understand me. Not yet. But this is hard country and cruel, and a person has to be a little like it to get along at all. A woman has got to know that a man is equal to anything in the life he asks her to share with him. Don't you see?"

"No," he said, "and thanks for the cake." He had not touched it, but he placed it on the bannister as he rose to a stand.

She only nodded and was not looking at him as he walked out to his waiting horse.

FOUR

Ute got back to Pick headquarters in the tail of the afternoon. He put up his horse and, seeing Loren's favorite white-stockinged mount in the day corral, he crossed at once to the ranch office. Loren was there, holding down Tap's chair again, with his boots hooked on the desk in the way that Tap used to sit and puzzle out his problems. Joe Lake was there, too.

"You see anything of Brig?" Ute asked.

Loren slowly lowered his feet to the floor and shook his head. "It looks like you might have been right, Ute. We found where he

49

swapped horses. We trailed him east a ways, and he was sure traveling. Moreover, we found a tag of your stuff up in the back graze. It had been run through the roughs."

"Brig ran it," Ute said. "I trailed that stuff, too. He took a few shots at me. I hit his horse. That's why he lit out, man. You'll never see anything more of him."

"I'm sure surprised," Loren said. "And it's funny you happened to catch him at it."

"Wanted me to," Ute returned. "He was some eager to kill me."

"Why on earth would he want to do that? Never had any trouble with him, did you?"

Ute shook his head. "He didn't need a quarrel. Just a chance. Which he or somebody went to some pains to set up. He got paid for it, Loren, or was going to."

Loren threw up his hands and gave Lake a look of complete, almost amused exasperation. He said, "Didn't I tell you this man's an Injun, Joe? He jumps a rustler, gets shot at, and right away somebody's trying to murder him. Who you scared of, Ute, anyhow?"

"Scared of nobody," Ute snapped. "And I'll cut the liver out of the next man that makes a try for me."

Loren sobered a little at that, then spread his hands in impatience. He said, "There you have it, kid. You're wild as they come. And sore because Tap realized it and took steps to protect Pick from you and your rambunctiousness. Next thing I know, you'll tell me I'm the one trying to get rid of you. As long as you stay single and acknowledge no offspring, I'm your heir. It works the other way, too, and don't you forget it. If I died, you'd be mine. That mean I ought to be suspicious of you?"

"Not suspicious," Ute said. "But don't under-rate me either, Loren. You remember that." He walked out, then, not trusting himself and knowing he had to take it slow and easy. There was Loren's marked-up map. He dared not forget it for a minute. His name had not been on that map, but there were a lot of other names. There was a special plan for him, but the two things tied together. He did not want Loren even remotely to guess how much he knew already.

During the next few days the matter seemed to have been forgotten. Round-up preparations now went ahead at full tilt. Word came from the adjoining spreads, from those who would furnish men and horses and from others who would only send reps. It was a cut-and-dried routine that followed the

51

same pattern year after year. Pick would send its wagons and the greater part of its crew to the south boundary line, which was also the lower edge of the Horseshoe. Although outmoded now, there was an old branding corral down there that Tap had used when help was scarcer than now.

The round-up would start at that point, and afterward the increasing beef gather would move north day by day. Weeks would be needed to cover the whole of Horseshoe Basin. Everyone was excited about it. The annual work brought together men who did not often see each other. It furnished hard but interesting toil in itself. Above all, it produced the beef that was the basin's sole income as well as permitting tallies of the herds and a reckoning of capital assets.

But this year there was to be a marked difference in round-up procedure. Ute did not discover that for sure until on the last evening before taking to the range. Joe Lake rapped the supper table for attention. That was his usual method of issuing general orders.

When all eyes had turned toward him, Lake spoke harshly: "I dunno just how it's going to shake down this year, boys. So I want an understanding with you before there's any showdown. Tap always threw the tall shadow in this country. He's gone. Let a big man drop out, and you'll find a lot of little ones getting big notions. We're apt to run into that. And we got to let the greasy-sackers know from the start that nothing's going to be different in the basin, even if Tap ain't here."

A look of astonishment had climbed onto Ute's face. He had never seen a thing to support the worry Lake was showing. So it must be Loren's worry, the fear that he might not be able to rule the basin with Tap's firm, sure hand.

"Pick's going to stay top dog," Lake was continuing. "Its help will back it right down the line or drag their hind ends over the hill. You all understand that?"

It was an order that would be wholly needless in the normal course of events. Man by man, the riders took it with a degree of wonder that was close to shock. Ute saw their puzzled eyes, their in-turned questioning. But heads slowly nodded, and not without resentment. No puncher worth his pay had to be forced to back his outfit. If he did not feel like doing so, he had the sense to call for his time, pack his war bag and hit the trail.

Ute did not like the look of it at all. Out of courtesy to Tap, either Loren or Lake was bound to be elected round-up boss. It sounded like they meant to get rough, from the very start, and were only making sure that they'd be backed in it strongly.

The chuck- and bed-wagons had gone out with the remuda. Right after an early breakfast, the next morning, the larger part of Pick's crew hit leather and noisily pointed themselves south. Ute could not help catching the spirit of it, and his worries were temporarily forgotten. By the time town people were sitting down to breakfast, the whole of Horseshoe Basin was assembled at Pick's old branding corral.

Ginny Ide was there. She had her own string of horses, a bed roll and a pair of pleased eyes. Herb Latamore was present, with one of his own riders, and Herb looked gloomy and quarrelsome. Ute greeted Herb and Ginny especially, for they came as close to being intimates of his as anybody in the whole crowd.

Heretofore the election of a round-up boss had been little more than a formality. Tap Taplan always had been chosen, with Tap naming Joe Lake his segundo. But there was a different feeling at this gathering, which Ute could not help but notice. It struck him that none of the men here liked Loren or wanted to work for him. But Pick was furnishing the chuck-wagon, and that in itself would settle the question.

It was Vic Rudeen who impatiently called for action, saying, "Well, boys, we'd better pick us a boss and get to riding. There's a lot of circles to be made before we hit my place, and I'm anxious to find out if I've finally gone broke. Old Tap's gone, and we'll have a hard time putting up a man who can fill his boots. Who we going to make it, this trip?"

"I say Ute Taplan," called a voice. It was Herb Latamore's, cold and firm.

The complete unexpectedness of that nomination stunned nine-tenths of those present. Ute blinked his eyes but could not help seeing Loren's cheeks pull stiff and the narrow way that Joe Lake looked at Herb. Pick's punchers stirred uneasily. Maybe this was what Lake had been getting at the night before — the first sign of rebellion in the basin. Maybe, they seemed to think, Lake had known what he was talking about. But it was not something that could be put down by force. The voting would be done by the owners.

Embarrassed but trying to be jocular about it, Rudeen said, "Him or Loren, since they're going to feed us. I'd say Loren. Any other nominations?"

Nobody said a thing.

Ute was on the point of declining, but he remembered that Olivia had said the basin preferred to see him on Pick and mother-henning the little ranches. The desire rose in him to see concrete evidence of that. But he doubted that Pick's neighbors would have the courage to vote against the man who now actually ran the big spread.

"We'll make it a written vote," Herb said, and he all but smiled.

Relief jumped into the faces of those who stood about so tensely.

"Now, just a minute," Joe Lake returned. "Ute's got no real standing as an owner. He's not eligible for the job."

"Neither are you," Herb retorted. "So shut up, Lake. I put up Ute's name, and you try and persuade me he ain't as much an owner as Loren. If he's willing, his name stays up."

"Why not?" Ute said on sudden impulse.

It took scrounging to scare up enough paper and pencils to have the vote. But the ballots were prepared and thoughtful men made their choice. The secret ballot seemed to encourage them, for none of them showed much hesitation in writing down his vote. Afterward Rudeen read off the votes, Stub Hines tallying them. The outcome wasn't even close. Loren got three votes, Ute eleven.

But nobody showed elation at that. The men looked disturbed over what they had done so unexpectedly. Loren only bit his lip, and he withheld his congratulations.

They rode a circle that forenoon and got the cutting started. Ute knew the grueling work so well that, at the start, the only requirement was sorting the men into the proper jobs. He understood the capabilities of each rider, almost of each horse. Outriders would work ahead of the main round-up, driving the scattered cattle out of the valleys and canyons, getting them in to where the main crew could handle them and complete the work.

In-riders compacted the herd on a holding ground, where beef steers and strays were cut out and where calves missed in the spring received the marking knife and branding iron. It was noisy, dusty, but satisfying toil which any other man there knew as well as Ute did. The job of a round-up boss was to coordinate the work, to settle disputes and plan ahead. In that respect, the cut of the man could make a vital difference.

The first day's work went forward without a hitch. Ute found within himself something of the sagacity of Tap, and for that reason he made Joe Lake his own segundo. Tap had always picked Lake since the man was his foreman, and that standing had not changed. Moreover, Ute was convinced that Herb Latamore sensed something disturbing to him and had tried to sledge it between the eyes with his surprise nomination. But Ute decided to give Loren and Lake a chance to do whatever they would have done otherwise just to see what happened. As straw boss, Lake would have some degree of opportunity. If anything happened to Ute now, Lake would step into his shoes.

Tired and dirty riders got their plates and cups and filed past the cook's table at supper time. Carrying his own food, Ute moved out of the circle of noisy men to where Herb was eating all by himself.

Dropping down beside Herb in an Indian's easy, cross-legged fashion, Ute said, "Why'd you do it, Herb?"

The man did not look up from his plate. He chewed the food in his mouth and swallowed it. Then he said, "I put up the man I wanted. What's wrong with that?"

"Risky, for one thing," Ute said. "You made an enemy out of the man who's going to run Pick. You encouraged ten other little basiners to do likewise. You had a reason, Herb. A real deep one, I think, because you're no fool."

"With you on Pick I ain't too inclined to worry," Herb said.

"I've got no say."

"You're a fool if you don't get yourself some say. Because you're going to be skinned out of everything if you don't. And it might not stop at that. You've got a responsibility to the rest of us. I showed you that, and I showed Loren where he stood. Ute, if you're worth your keep, you'll meet it."

"Herb, I won't be on Pick at all," Ute said. "I bought the old Rocking A from Chance Donner. Moving over right after round-up's finished."

Now Herb looked up from his food to give Ute a piercing stare. "You're breaking with Pick completely?"

"I'm through."

"Then," said Herb, "there's hell to pay."

"Why do you think so, Herb? What are you scared of?"

"I'm scared of a born hog," Herb said. "But this is no place to talk about it. You're boss of this round-up, anyhow. I'll feel all right as long as you can set a saddle." Then, his eyes softening a little, "Ute, I know it hit you pretty hard the way it turned out. Not getting any say in Pick was getting kind of disowned."

"Herb, to your mind am I the kid Tap lost?"

"No," Herb said promptly.

That hit Ute harder than Herb's surprise nomination at the election. "Sounds like you made up your mind as to that a long time ago," he said. "How come?"

"You ain't like either one of them," Herb said. "You were only a wild Injun when they brought you to Pick. Never was a mystery to me why Tap was dubious. Nor why you went all out when finally you switched your affections to him. And to Olivia."

"Where does she come in?"

Herb put down his plate and fished for tobacco and papers. "She was only your age, but the only female around. She took the place of the mother you'd known, just as Tap did the father. What I'm trying to say, Ute, is that you hadn't ought to mistake the nature of either set of feelings. You never were a Taplan to my mind. You ain't a bit like Tap or Loren, and in a lot of ways they were identical. I voiced my opinion of what you are when I nominated you for round-up boss."

In a temper-roughened voice, Ute said, "Tap was as good as they come."

"He was a good cowman," Herb agreed.

Ute had not finished his plate, but he had no appetite left. Instead he was aware of an all-gone feeling. It came partly from Herb's quick opinion, never before asked, as to his identity. The rest came from Herb's thinly veiled disapproval — never expressed before, either — of Tap Taplan. And there was a third source, he realized, for Herb had tried to tell him he was mixed up about Olivia and his feeling for her, as well.

FIVE

The discovery of Herb Latamore's dubiety as to his origin left Ute sick at heart. Maybe he was pure Indian and had no business being here at all but should be living on the Black Rock with his people. Maybe, and the thought was a more deadly poison in his emotion, he was the result of some Indian woman's lying under the stars with a white man to earn a pittance. An accident, sprung out of a cheap commerce.

That probability — which seemed supported by his features and yellow hair — hit him hard and haunted him. It tightened the lines of his face and put back some of the wildness they all claimed had once been in his eyes. It turned him dangerous in a situation that was already fraught with danger enough.

The beef gather went forward steadily and without a hitch. While part of the crew rode circle, the rest cut the big herd that never seemed to grow smaller in consequence because of the continual influx from the open range. Of the separate cuts growing on nearby holding grounds, Pick's market steers were the largest part. But also strays from the other ranches were cut out and turned over to the various representatives.

When this section of the basin had been worked out, the operation moved forward, going north. Now and then there was a tangle over a maverick or over somebody's careless work, but nothing serious. Either Ute or Lake did the refereeing, and both were impartial. It began to look like Loren and Lake had set aside whatever it was that had caused Lake to demand loyalty before it was needed from Pick's own crew.

The weather made an abrupt change. One day's intense heat gave way to coolness. Toward evening of the second day, heavy clouds scudded in from the southwest. It rained all that night and through the next day, while the temper of the whole crew changed to surliness. In spite of tarps and the dubious shelter of the wagon beds, nobody had slept dry and comfortable except Ginny Ide, who occupied the hooligan wagon for privacy. The night herders had sat wet saddles, and everyone had soggy leather to fork for the day. The crew ate breakfast standing about in the slippery gumbo mud, looking sour and edgy.

Even the horses were waspish, that morning, pitching at the touch of wet blankets and saddles, and again when riders stepped up. The morning's work was difficult, vexatious. The soggy hair of the steers made the brands hard to read. Wood for the fires was wet. The cutting horses had trouble keeping their feet. The steers themselves rebelled at the rougher handling and turned pugnacious.

Instead of the weather clearing up, a second downpour started at noon. Ute was tempted to call a halt until it was over. But at this time of the year things had to move on schedule. The beef cut, the market drive, and then the preparations for a winter that would wait on no one. He kept the outfit going through a grueling and miserable afternoon.

He rode in to supper to make the discovery that Olivia Latamore had ridden out, disdaining the bad weather. It had been to see Herb, apparently, and now Olivia stood at the cook's fire trying to dry out and soak up some heat. But the long ride through the rough elements seemed only to have exhilarated her. Her cheeks were colored, and she appeared to be enjoying herself.

Ute turned his mount over to the wrangler and went to wash the mud off his hands and face. He saw that Olivia was quietly watching him. That pleased him, for they had parted the last time in mutual temper and he had been unhappy about that ever since. He crossed over to her, saying, "The man was right about there being some good in every wind. Glad you come up."

She gave him a quick look, with a smile breaking, and he guessed she was as relieved as he that there would be no lingering resentments. If Herb thought his feeling for her was like a child's for its mother, Herb was crazy. Ute had never wanted more strongly to take her into his arms. For some reason the sting went out of what Herb had said on that one score.

"Had to see Dad," Olivia said easily. "And I hear they made you round-up boss this year."

Obviously that had pleased her. Ute nodded. "The boys decided to work under a handicap, this trip. You going to stay up here all night? I reckon Ginny's got room in the hooligan wagon for you."

"I've got to get home."

"Come and eat, then. I'll ride a piece with you afterward."

He got Olivia a plate of food and a cup of coffee. She ate standing, and as soon as he could afterward, he got horses and they started out. By any man's book it was a miserable evening, but he felt wonderful. When they had lost the camp.behind, he said, "Herb tell you I'm quitting Pick after round-up?"

She said, "Yes."

"You don't like it?"

"I think it's crazy, and I think it's weak."

There it was, back between them again, and he knew that she would never go to the old Arbuckle place to live with him as he had hoped all along. The shock of seeing this so plainly was as bad as having Herb set Tap up in a wholly new and unflattering light.

Gruffly he said, "And have you shared Herb's opinion that I'm no Taplan at all?"

"What difference does that make?" she asked. "Tap acknowledged you in the will, at least, and I think you're being extremely unwise about the rest."

"Which is pretty good for a bastard that probably came into being when nothing

65

more than a cheap looking-glass changed hands."

She gave him a quick, startled look, almost frightened. Then a sudden sympathy flooded her eyes the way it used to do when they were much younger. She said, "Ute, I know what it must be like to be in such complete doubt about yourself. But Tap always said the Paiutes told him they got you off an emigrant train. So you must be all white. There's as good a chance that you had fine parents as otherwise. Don't brood about it so much. Please."

He stopped his horse and reached out and stopped hers. They were back where they used to be, back where she had helped him out of his troubledness and depressions and enabled him to see things straight. He guessed that was all she was trying to do in urging him to go to law against Loren, if necessary. Herb had felt the same way about that. She was only trying to help get him on the track again.

Softly she said, "I think I know why you want to go on the old Rocking A. If you can build it into a successful ranch, the way Tap built one, you'll have proved you're his son."

"You think that's foolish, though."

"Isn't it? You're a rich man, already — if you'll fight for your own. Don't you see?

Loren feels he's got to justify Tap's judgment, just as you want to dispute it. I don't see any reason for either of you to go down in ruin just to prove points like that."

"Livvy, you know I love you. In your heart, you don't think I'm any quitter at all. You just don't like the course I picked. But I got to do it. It's all-fired important to me."

"I know, Ute."

He watched her through the murky dusk, thinking of something else that he did not presently want to discuss. Herb had told him not to mistake his feeling for her. He was remembering now that, the last time he saw her, Olivia had said that she was not certain as to the real nature of her feeling for him. He knew that he had always held her in a kind of reverence that had kept him from many an aggression he might otherwise have made. But what was wrong with that?

Then, as if suspecting the turn of his thoughts, she said, "You've got to work tomorrow. You'd better go back and get your rest."

Her slickered shape was slim in the saddle. Her face, under her rainhat, was a tantalizing obscurity.

He bent over, but she only laughed and said, "Don't drown me." And then she was gone.

Loren was in the group at the campfire. The moment Ute strode up after leaving his horse at the remuda, he was aware of the sudden storminess of the man's eyes. For the first time the real cogency of the fact that he had taken to calling on Olivia came to the fore for Ute. He had never given much thought to where Loren's interest in the matter of women might lie.

He's trying to take over everything I've got, Ute thought, and in the same flash he saw the deadly depths of the competition between them. In Loren's lights they both were pretenders to the throne that Tap had vacated. By completely dispossessing the man he disclaimed as a brother, Loren seemed to hope he could remove the last danger to his own prestige. And then Ute had the disturbing memory of the change so apparent in Olivia lately. She was still on his side but egging him on in a course he knew he would never follow. He was suddenly doubtful, even fearful, of the final effect of that on Olivia Latamore.

Loren gave him that one long, penetrating stare, then turned away. Ute looked at the other men at the fire and said, "The bunch seems jumpy to me, tonight. We won't be able to work it if this weather keeps up. Where's Joe?"

"Lake rode off somewhere," Whitey Marbow said tiredly.

The gusty wind slapped at the canvas sheets of the bedwagon where Ginny slept. The rain was sporadic, sometimes splattering down and again dwindling. Ute sent a couple of extra men out to the herd. He did not see Herb Latamore, then remembered that the man was already out there on night guard.

Ute was trying to find a place to spread his tarp and soggy blankets when the trouble came, catching him flat-footed. Lightning was the thing that usually exploded a herd, and there had been none in this storm. But there was a sudden, unearthly racket of some sort off on the holding grounds. Instantly the herd's grumbling became louder, menacing.

No man in the cow camp needed orders. Punchers shoved up automatically, tired but driven. They bolted into the darkness toward the remuda. Ute lunged blindly ahead of them, hearing the increased bawling of the cattle and continuing to detect that queer racket. The night hawk was doing his best to provide mounts but it was not good enough. Punchers threaded into the horse band trying to get leather under them. Somehow Ute found a horse and

69

swung aboard.

The stampede had started before he was away from the camp. It was one of the berserk kind in which the herd simply blew apart. It had taken some terrible scare to do that, which Ute already knew to have been the weird noise. The cattle were peeling in every direction, going down in the mud and piling over each other. Ute dug in his spurs, driving his horse heedlessly forward. There would be no stopping the thing. The steers had to work the travel out of themselves. The one hope was to keep them in some sort of cohesion, bending the run around so that it stayed in the clearway and milled until it was run down.

The wild alarm went out of Ute as he settled to the job. Other horses were thundering behind him, while off to the left streaked the shapes of countless cattle. They had developed something of a grain in this vicinity, all of this part of the herd running in the same general direction. Ute swung in closer. He pulled up his pistol. But at first horses and riders sought only to flank the herd. Ute kept flogging his own mount, trying to reach the point. Somebody had to throw himself and horse at that mad, onrushing front end to try to deflect and gradually turn it back upon the racing mass behind. In assuming that responsibility, Ute was only doing what any other puncher in the outfit would have done.

There was no shooting yet. Horses and cattle thundered on. From out of the black sky came a drenching downpour of rain, but no helpful light. Ute thought that he was gaining the point of the maddened herd when he became aware of another horse coming up behind and gaining on him fast. There were horses in his own string that could not be come upon in that wise, but now he forked the one he had been able to get in the scramble at the remuda.

Then a gun blazed out, its flash making an instant of light. Ute felt something hit and nearly drive him out of the saddle. He flattened, forward, his arms clasping the neck of the horse. There was another shot from behind him. Then the rearward horse swung out and fell back. All down the line guns blazed out, the harried punchers taking those two shots for a signal to tie into the herd.

Ute straightened in the saddle and slowed his plunging horse. He was hit in the shoulder, and that was all he knew for the moment. He still gripped his .45 in his good right hand. He whipped his horse around so fast that it skidded in the mud and nearly went down. Somebody else was coming on well down from him firing over the herd and shouting. The attacker's horse had faded outward into the drenched night. He had made his try, and if it had been good the thing would have been set down to an accident resulting from the guns now exploding all about, fired only for the effect of their sound upon the herd and the diverting influence of the flame streaks.

Ute was numb and shaken, but the emergency kept him going. Other riders had whipped past him by then, following the herd. Men shouted and fanned their hats. They reloaded and again emptied their pistols. Reaction hit Ute finally, causing him to sag in the saddle. This had been planned, probably from the start of the bad weather that had turned men and cattle so restive. Something had been sent into the herd to spook it. Ute meant to find out what, and he intended to determine the man who had shot him. In the back. That fact about it was the deepest part of his cold and consuming anger.

Somehow Ute got back into it, and somehow he kept saddle through the rest of that mad run. *The cattle first* was more than an axiom; it was instinct in a range-bred man. The herd was still in the open, still running in free stride. But Ute grew aware that the men who had got ahead of him were bending the point at last. Afterward physical forces would take over. The steers would have died, and maybe men and horses with them. That was the toll of the fierce, fatalistic phenomenon of a cattle stampede.

At long last the herd was in a discernible mill, and then Ute fell out, having to hold to the saddlehorn to stay on his horse. The crisis subsiding, he was thawing out himself, and pain was a hot sear through the whole left side of him. He was not sure how far he had come from the cow camp but knew that it must have been miles. Assured that the cattle would be all right, he started back in. He was sure as hell an Indian. He meant to cut the heart out of the man who had caused all this tonight.

Even the cook had got a horse, and Ute found that he was the first one to return to camp. He slid out of the saddle, tried to walk to the guttering fire. He hadn't gone half the distance when the streaming earth swung up and hit him hard. That was the last he knew . . .

It was a queer thing that it should be Loren's anxious face above him when he opened his eyes.

"What happened to you, kid?" Loren was saying.

It took a moment for Ute to get his throat to work. "Somebody was careless with a shooting iron." That was all he was going to say to Loren, as yet, and maybe to anybody else. Let the story that would have been told had the shots made good be told anyway and let it prevail until the truth could come out in its naked ugliness. There was a round-up on. There were angry men to hold together.

"What the hell made that racket at the start?" he added. "Anybody find out?"

"Nobody knows," Loren said. "Except that it raised billy hell. Herb Latamore's horse went down. He's hurt, and worse than you are."

"Herb?"

"The hills across the herd from where you were, run close to the creek," Loren explained. "The steers crowded Herb over the bank. He spilled with his horse and hit hard."

"How do you know which side of the herd I was on, Loren?"

Loren's shoulders pulled straight. Then he said, "You had to be on the near side or you couldn't have been the first one back to camp. That was a queer question. Why'd you ask it? Is that Injun coming up in you again? Figure I tried to do you in?"

"Some jumpy rider just got careless," Ute said, growing aware then of something, hard to grasp because of its enormity. The stampede had been man-made — there was no question in his mind about that. He and Herb Latamore had been hurt in it. It was dawning on him in slow horror that Herb's Crosscut had been labeled with a number one, on Tap's map and in Loren's hand.

"We sent a man after a doctor for you two," Loren was continuing. "Don't worry. Joe will take over the round-up. We'll get you down to the ranch."

Don't worry — don't worry . . . Ute thought, and then the black swirls wiped out his awareness again.

When he opened his eyes the next time he discovered that he was under the bed-wagon, heavily covered with blankets. His gaze fell on Ginny, who sat beside him.

"Herb?" he gasped, and that was as much as he could get out.

"Now, you just be quiet, Ute," Ginny said. "You pushed yourself too far while you were losing too much blood."

"I'm all right."

"You will be if you'll use sense. Oh, Ute — I died a hundred times last night."

Ignoring her worried protests, he worked himself to a sit. The rain had stopped, he observed, with the drenching surface water soaked in to furnish a firmer footing. The camp was empty except for the cook stolidly going about his work. Out in the distance was the horse wrangler. Then he saw something else that was like the touch of fire on his neck. Something lay under a canvas out there, a little apart from the camp itself.

He said, "Oh, God," in the faintest way.

Ginny nodded. "Herb passed away, Ute. Somebody went down to bring up a buckboard to take him home."

But he could only sit and stare at the shape out there. He finally got to a rocking stand. His first want was to see Olivia and try to help her somehow. But nobody had to tell him he could not stick a horse long enough to ride down to Crosscut. Maybe they would let him go in the rig with Herb's body.

He said, "Well, what else went wrong?"

"The herd came through pretty well," Ginny answered as if anxious to get his mind off its centering thought. "But the beef cut and strays got clear away. The round-up work, so far, is wiped out. We'll have to start over, and you'll have to turn it over to Joe Lake. Isn't that odd, when Joe tried so hard to get Loren elected boss instead of you?"

He swung to stare at her in hard intention. Harshly he said, "Ginny, you keep a dally on your tongue. I reckon I know what you mean. And if we're right, lives are held cheap in this outfit. Don't make talk that would be dangerous to anybody, Ginny. Don't you do it. I'll have to set out the next week or so. And I think you'd better quit and go home."

"Why?"

"I think they know already that you're suspicious — the same as Herb was. Only I think there was more than that connected with what happened to him. I can't tell you about it. Don't ask me."

He got some coffee and drank it, trying to build up strength he knew would not be quick in coming back to him. The shock of his wound, the blood loss, the subexhaustion into which he had driven himself in the night had taken far too much out of him.

He had barely put down the cup when he saw Loren and Lake ride in. The ramrod carried something, and as they came up to where Ute stood Lake's face showed a cool grin. He held a string of tin cans, which he tossed to the ground in front of Ute.

"There's what started the run," he said.

"Somebody tin-canned a yearling and drove it into the herd. The critter went down and was tramped to death. These jingle bells were still tied to its tail. Me and Loren just found it." Lake gave him a long, bland stare. "If you want my opinion, it was that damned drifter, Brig."

"Spite work?" Ute said.

Loren shook his head. "An old rustling caper. He tried to whittle on you up on Broken Back, didn't he? Ute, I've got a feeling that he was no lone wolf. He didn't run your steers off, remember. He only spotted them where they could be picked up easy later. There's a gang backing Brig. I'd bet on it. And now we've donated them a week's work, to say nothing of a cut of select beef that makes your little bunch look piddling. That beef cut's scattered from here to hell and mighty easy pickings for a gang of rustlers."

"Well, it's your round-up for a while," Ute said to Lake. "What are you going to do about it?"

"That's what we come to see you about," Loren replied for Lake. "Joe will have to run the show till you can ride again. Me, I'd like to take some of my own boys and flush the malpais before we do any more work for them buzzards. Meanwhile, you'll

78

have to go down to Pick and take it easy. We figured Ginny had better drop out and go home, too. This business is getting too rough for a woman."

"I figure that way myself," Ute said. "But you'll have to order her to do it."

"I'll order her," Lake said promptly.

SIX

The doctor arrived in midmorning. He had been asked to come up there mainly because of Herb whose injury had made it dangerous for him to be moved. Now, with Herb dead, the medico had only Ute's shoulder to dress, which he did while he confirmed Ute's fears. Continuing with the round-up was out of the question for many days ahead. Ute got his roll and rode down to Pick headquarters in the doctor's buggy, not feeling up to accompanying Herb in the buckboard and going at once to see Olivia.

He did not know what had happened to Ginny until she showed up at Pick on the following morning. He was at the cook shack, mixing cigarettes and coffee into an effort to figure things out, when he saw her ride in. He strode to the door at once. She looked grave, irritable and deeply concerned.

"The world's gone crazy," he said. "I figured they'd have trouble sending you home. But it looks like you gave in without a struggle, for once. I never expected to see that, Ginny."

But she was in no mood for banter. "Ute, I'm scared to death." She swung down, in a skirt this morning, a small, trim and appealing shape. "What puncher would be so careless as to hit a man the way you were shot?"

"Somebody was."

"Somebody did it on purpose," Ginny said fiercely. "I've tried to talk myself out of it, but I can't. I almost came right out and said it to you yesterday. I think they tried to kill you — that they did kill Herb. That's why I'm scared. You watch yourself better."

"Been watching," he said. "But a man don't always know where."

"I've got to go on," Ginny told him. "I stayed with Olivia last night. The funeral will be today. She asked me to get the word around."

"How's she taking it?"

"I don't know. It's always hard to tell what she's feeling."

Ute was beginning to realize for himself what a fact that was. He had risen that morning intending to have a buggy hitched up for him so he could drive over to Cross-cut. But he had kept putting it off so far, not quite knowing why he did.

Ginny went up to the saddle, although Ute was about ready to talk the whole thing over with her, even if it did involve so many unproven suspicions about his supposed brother. She had a level head, a clear vision, and might be able to help him. It was Ginny's own welfare that dissuaded him. Loren and Lake had been anxious to send her home from the round-up. He had no right to lend support to what she must already be guessing, for there were times when she could be as impetuous as himself. He kept still and let her ride out.

A couple of Pick's old retainers were on hand to take care of things at headquarters while the crew was away on the round-up. They hitched up the buckboard, and all three of them drove over to Crosscut for the funeral. There was a big turnout for Herb's last rites. Women had come over from the different ranches. Ginny had got word to the round-up crew, which was there in force. It did not take long, and the crowd dispersed much more swiftly than it had assembled.

Because he had not yet seen Olivia alone, Ute remained behind. They sat in Crosscut's little parlor, Olivia shocked, bewildered but dry-eyed. He tried to dredge up some way he could help her through the hard period. But there wasn't much anybody could do.

He said, "I been turned out to pasture for a week or so, Olivia. If there's anything at all I can do for you, I'll sure jump at the chance."

"Thank you, Ute." Olivia's voice was low but steady. She had ought to break down and cry and get it out of her system. But she never would. She had a manlike fear of showing weakness, he remembered. She was pretty guarded about all of her emotions.

"I can't think of anything," she said. "I've got to go in and see Chance Donner and find out how things stand at the bank. Dad never talked about his business."

"Could I drive you in? I could use some things from town, myself."

"Why, I'd like that. But not for a day or so."

"How about Friday?" he asked and, at her nod, added, "I'll be over and pick you up."

He went back to Pick feeling washed-out and temperish. Loren or Lake had swung by headquarters, and when Ute looked in the drawer of Tap's desk he found that the marked map of Horseshoe Basin was gone. They had been afraid he would get to poking around and come across it. He puzzled at that, but it was a scramble of pieces until Loren had shown more of his intentions.

Loren rode into headquarters on Thursday evening. He was assured, amiable, looking wholly satisfied with the way things were shaping up. "Well, I never had much luck in the malpais," he told Ute. "But we seen enough sign to justify our suspicions. There's rustlers in there, with the odds ten to one Brig's one of them. We'll keep our weather eye open from now on."

"What kind of sign?"

"Stuff's been run through there, and on out the far side of the roughs. You should have brought your cut down from Broken Back. The whole shebang's gone now."

"No!" Ute gasped. The steers were his only hope of starting up on Rocking A. With them gone, he was out of business already.

But Loren was talking again, saying, "While I was gone, Joe got the round-up going again. Dunno how we'll ever tell what we lost in that stampede, though it's a cinch it was plenty. But we're taking no chances on them trying that again. Joe's got the night guard doubled. And we've decided not to start anything moving to the railroad till round-up's finished and the whole lot can trail together. I offered to let the greasysackers hold their trail cuts on our grass."

"That would sure be rustler bait," Ute commented.

"Bait, maybe," Loren agreed. "But we've been warned. This basin wants its beef checks. Any rustlers had better come armed to the teeth the next time."

"If the basin never got any beef checks," Ute said, "it would be right up the creek, wouldn't it?"

"It sure would. We couldn't take a loss like that, ourselves. That's why I come down to talk about it. Ute. Soon as you're able, you can take over guarding the trail herd."

"Soon as I'm able," Ute retorted, "I'm coming back to the job I was elected to do."

"All right. But if you ask me, the trail herd is going to be the hottest to handle."

Ute could have chewed the hind leg off a bear after that. He wanted to ride up to Broken Back and see for himself, yet he did not doubt that Loren had told the truth about his stocker steers having been rustled for sure. He went to bed fuming and he was still fuming when he got up the next morning. Except for his agreement to take Olivia into Starbow, he would have endured the pain of riding to Broken Back to make his own investigation.

Yet he wanted to see Olivia, too, to be with

her through the greater part of that day. He shaved and put on his best clothes and got a clean cloth for his arm sling. He had the buckboard hitched up and then drove off for Crosscut through the early morning sunshine. It was a fine day that began to draw him out of himself. Mornings of this season had a touch of coolness. The hard glare of summer was gone, with distances soft and purple and inviting to the eye. The year's fullness of fertility was falling behind. Nesters were taking in the last of their crops. The beef gather was shaping up, at least, and the cowmen, as everyone else, were turning their thoughts to winter.

At Crosscut Olivia was ready and waiting, still grave but recovering a little from the first stunning impact of her loss. Ute helped her swing into the buckboard seat, a sheer gallantry with a range woman, then settled himself beside her. She was quiet, and he made no effort to break in upon that privacy.

They reached town in midmorning. When he had let Olivia out at the bank, Ute drove on along the street until he found an empty space at a tie rack. He went first to the doctor's office to have his shoulder dressed. It was coming along fine, he was told. He could put it to work as soon as the soreness would permit. Thereafter, he picked up some tobacco and shells.

He went to the Rialto for a drink only to find that the place could not hold his interest nor the whiskey lift his spirits. So he wound up in a round-back chair on the hotel porch. He had been there only a few minutes when Johnny Dunson came hobbling along the sidewalk.

Johnny was a gaffer who had quit the range to live in town with a married daughter, and he never missed a chance to talk with somebody in from the sagebrush.

"Howdy, Ute," he called as he climbed the steps. "I hear tell that you bought the Arbuckle place. What you figure to do out there — live on jack rabbit?"

"Might have to," Ute admitted. "Sit down, Johnny."

The old man took the next chair. "You know," he began reminiscently, "when I first hit this country, that old place was as good as any around. Then it lost its water."

"How'd that happen?" Ute asked. He had never heard that said before.

Johnny Dunson gave him a curious glance. "Well, it was before your time, Ute. And you wouldn't be apt to hear, afterward, that Tom Arbuckle never went busted till Pick took his crick away from him."

"Pick — a crick?"

"There was a time," said Johnny, "when the Twist was the main crick out there. You know how that stream splits and runs down through the deltas. One branch is the Twist, t'other the Jackdaw. Pick had frontage on the Jackdaw, Arbuckle on the Twist, with the deltas between. Pick owned the deltas, too. But you must know all that."

Ute shook his head. "Most of Tap's business was locked up in his head. But I always though the Jackdaw was our eastern boundary."

"Huh-uh. The old Twist channel is. I ought to know. Arbuckle fumed to me plenty about that little caper of Tap Taplan's. The way things stood, Tap had plenty of access to water for all the range he had in there. All the Jackdaw and half of the Twist, if he wanted to put his stuff across the deltas. But that didn't satisfy him. It was hard to have to water all the time by driving across the deltas. There were some cross sloughs that were stagnant and dangerous to steers. Then Tap got his big break."

"What happened?"

"Flood water, one winter. When it was over the Jackdaw was running most of the water. Things like that happen in country where the soil's sandy enough. Snags or something plugged the Twist a little, and the Jackdaw started scouring out."

"The course of nature," Ute said. "What made you say it was a caper of Tap's?"

"Arbuckle swore to the day he died that dynamite pinched off the Twist during that flood. It was storming like hell, but he thought he heard an explosion one night. Then the water went down, with the normal flow all running on Pick and Tom Arbuckle cut off."

"Guesswork on Arbuckle's part," Ute snapped, not liking the light Johnny was trying to throw on Tap.

"Mebbeso," Johnny agreed. "But what kind of a man would refuse the way Tap did to let any part of that water be turned back into its old bed?"

"He refused?"

"Flat. He let Tom go broke. He let others come in afterward and try to make it on wells and go broke, too. What always gravelled me was that Pick already had plenty of water. It just didn't like to have its stuff drifting through the deltas. Filling the Jackdaw stopped that. Tap got him a fence, kind of, that Tom paid for with his spread."

"Johnny," Ute said narrowly. "Why are you telling me this?"

"Not to blacken the name of your dead

father," Johnny said. "But I seen Herb Lata-more one day when he was in town just before round-up started. He told me about your fears that you ain't Tap's real kid. Like Herb — well, I reckon I figure you hadn't ought to feel too bad about that, Ute. Nobody would say anything around you before. Wouldn't now, except for the mix-up you're in."

"Well, thanks."

"And another thing. It kind of struck me that if you knew how Rocking A lost its water, you might see how to put it back."

"Johnny, I already had an idea along that line."

Johnny changed the subject, then, and presently he hobbled off.

Ute sat there a long while, wondering how many other corners Tap had cut in his time. It was not a pleasant curiosity, and the lines of his face hardened. He had more reason than ever to try to restore the old Arbuckle ranch. He would do it, and Olivia nor anybody else could turn him from it. He would make it or go broke on the old spread that Pick had so callously ruined.

He had been watching the bank, and it was not long until he saw Olivia emerge onto the sidewalk. She had said that she had trading to do afterward, and she went on into Trowe's store. Ute gave her more time, then got the buckboard and drove up in front of the mercantile.

She came out quietly, giving him a grave smile, and they started home. But they were halfway back to Crosscut before she made mention of what she had learned of the business affairs she now had to handle by herself. Ute did not care to know, unless she wanted to share her troubles with him.

At last she said, "Well, it's not too bad. But not good, either. I know that Dad worried a lot in recent months. But he wasn't inclined to talk business with me. There's a mortgage in arrears and a note he gave Donner to cover an overdue payment. The note's due right after the beef drive. It won't leave much for me to run on. Donner suggested that I lay off one of my boys. But I can't do that. They've worked for us for years."

Ute didn't figure that it was in Donner to worry much about two old cowhands being laid off. Dropping a hand over hers, he said, "Don't let it worry you, Livvy. You'll make out. And if it's rough going, you'll have company. I'm beginning to realize how tough a row I picked myself to hoe."

"You're still planning on moving over to Rocking A?"

"I'm more determined than ever. Seen Johnny Dunson while I was waiting in town. He says Pick broke that spread. Tom Arbuckle with it. Johnny still resents that, and I don't blame him a bit. I guess there were things like that in your dad's craw, too. Things he seen coming out all over again in Loren."

"He never liked Loren," Olivia admitted.

"But you do?"

"Well, I do," she answered promptly. "I've told you before, Ute, that a person's got to be hardheaded to get on the top. I'd rather see a man too much that way than too soft."

"You really think I'm soft?"

"Too soft to fill the job you resent Loren's having. I'm sorry, Ute, but it's something we've got to get straightened out." Olivia put an impulsive hand on his and smiled up at him.

But he was still stung by her persistent references to that side of him.

Aware of that, she added, "I do like you, Ute. An awful lot."

"You've already chopped it down from the love I thought it was."

"Ute, we never had any understanding."

"You want one now? You want to make it clear there'll be nothing between us unless I see and do things your way? Tell me something. Would you marry me if I could set you up as the mistress of Pick?"

"Probably. But not because of that, alone. Only because it would be proof that you're a fighting man. I don't mean in physical courage. You've got that. It's more a matter of moral courage — the determination to fight for what you think is right."

"What do you think I'm doing?"

"It's not right for you to let yourself be cut out of your full inheritance."

"The hell with the inheritance," he exploded. "Loren can have it all."

"That's what I was afraid you'd say. I'm sorry, Ute. But everything has changed, and I've got to get my bearings."

Things welled on his tongue that he knew he dared not say to her. Suspicions of how her father had really died, suspicions of what was coming to all the basin — but suspicions only. And there was another need in him for silence on that score. It was the old test again, the weighing of himself against Loren. She had to make up her own mind about everything. That was the only way it would ever come out right.

"You're telling me to forget about us?" he asked.

"For a while."

"I won't let you go to Loren."

"You mean you'll fight?"
"Wait and see."

SEVEN

To remain in enforced idleness on Pick was unbearable to Ute. His healing shoulder was tender enough to hamper the free use of his restless body. Energies manufactured by his healthy flesh roiled in him without outlet, engendering a physical malaise as troublesome as the worries that gnawed at his mind.

But he found that by having a horse saddled for him he could manage to swing up to the leather seat and get about at a careful pace. Thus he chose to make the long ride to Broken Back, taking all the day for it. He had in part accepted Loren's report that his stockers had vanished from up there. He had rejected only Loren's account of the rustling and who was behind it.

Arrived on the backland meadow, he scouted about and found new sign so abundant that the suspicion rose instantly that it had been planted. In his physical condition there was little more that he could do about it at the present time. Yet he spent long moments staring out across the sunburned sweep of the malpais.

Out there was an endless variety of terrain. There were many places where one renegade or a whole wild bunch could hide out indefinitely. Also there were some places he knew of where rustled cattle could be held for a considerable time. Loren and Lake had been quick to shape up the theory that the little man Brig was at the head of, or an important part in, such a gang. Yet Ute was deeply convinced that Brig was far from being the prime moving force in the obscure operations, which had occurred not only here on Broken Back but on the round-up.

He wished fervently that he was in condition to ride on into the badlands and make some private observations. Yet that was out of the question. He had to admit that and continue the hard effort of biding his time.

Leaving Broken Back, he rode down upon the Jackdaw at the point where it broke off from Twist Creek and made its own way down the country. The Jackdaw branch was the younger stream, he knew now from what he had been told by Johnny Dunson. From the wide, stagnant bed of the Twist it was easy to see now that it had once been as large as its companion stream. Both channels were full of meanders, shifting their course this way and that in the loose soil. For the length of the Jackdaw the divided channels ran past a narrow delta of little islands for a reach of several miles. Finally the stream beds joined up again.

He rode on to visit the old spread's headquarters. This time it looked to be what people had always claimed — a sorry proposition. Yet, as he poked around the place, his jaw began to set in a new firmness. He had reached his low in spirit, in hopes and in position. He had wanted to start at the bottom and knew now that he had found a deeper bottom than he had figured on. Yet he had sense enough to realize that was probably to the good. The shakedown, the opening of his eyes to facts he had never before suspected, had sobered him and made him understand the grimness of the course he had chosen to follow.

The next morning, over coffee in the cook shack with old Jeb Flanders, Ute said, "Jeb, you worked for Tap a long time. Were you around when Twist Creek plugged up and the Jackdaw got the water?"

Flanders was one of Pick's retainers, a cowhand grown too old for the saddle who now wrangled, chored about the spread and at times relieved the cook who was now off on round-up. A gaunt man with a long and skinny face, he was short-and-seldom spoken, revealing his inner nature only through his outward habits.

He scowled a little at Ute's question, and for a moment afterward seemed to put it closely through his mind. Then all he said was, "Yeah, I was around. Why?"

"Just what happened?"

"The upper crick overflowed, that's all. When the water went down, things were changed."

"Jeb, I heard tell that sometime during that storm, Tom Arbuckle figured he heard dynamite go off in the night."

"Heard the same story."

"What do you think of it?"

"Why," said Jeb, "I think he probably did."

"You know damned well he did."

"All right. Ought to know. I heard it planned. I seen some of the boys go out with dynamite that night. Next day the crick was on a new course."

Thoughtfully, Ute said, "Why did you admit it, Jeb?"

"I always liked you. Know how you been feeling. Don't mind helping to cure you."

"Lots of others have felt the same way, I guess," Ute said. He had believed old Johnny, who was talkative but no liar, yet had felt a need to get confirmation of that story if he could.

"But forget I told you," Jeb said. "Me, I've got too damned old to risk my job."

"Well," Ute said, "a pea shooter can be blown from either end. Maybe Loren's going to learn that."

Jeb Flanders only shrugged.

Ute endured another week of idleness and at the end of that time pronounced himself fit again. Except for a tender lameness, he had good use of his hurt shoulder and arm. He could at least ride without pain. One morning he saddled a horse without help and, thus encouraged, headed out at once for the round-up operation.

The work had progressed for a considerable distance up the basin, he found, but was still on Pick's vast range. Early in the day as it was, cutting work was already going on at the herd. Under the fly at the chuck-wagon, the cook was repairing the wreckage — the litter of dishes and utensils left after the morning meal. Joe Lake apparently had gone out with the circle riders. Neither he nor Loren was in sight.

Stub Hines was tallying. He said, "Howdy, Ute. Damn your eyes, I hope you're back on the job."

"What's wrong, Stub?" Ute said.

"What's right?" Stub retorted. "You never

seen such a bunch of soreheads in your life
as this outfit. Lake's sure running the
round-up — him and Loren. The rest of us
don't know what's going on. We just take
orders. Some of 'em sound funny, too. While
we're on Pick, we got to take that. But once
we get on up the country, there's apt to be
a showdown. Unless you're back before
then."

"Back already," Ute said. "What's been
going on?"

"Well," Stub said, "Joe, he started riding
us rough-shod the day you left. He goes out
of his way to be galling. He's even got some
of Pick's own riders sore about it, although
it's us peewee ranchers he lays it onto."

"That'll stop," Ute promised. "Is Joe out
on circle?"

"Dunno where he is. But I'd sure like to
see his face when you tell him you're ready
to relieve him. Nobody looked for you back
for another week or so. Ute —" Hines
hesitated, then, "I just want to say you can
figure on us little hombres backing you,
straight down the line. Makes me ashamed,
the sneaky way we had to vote for you in
secret. A break's coming, and we might as
well of had it there. Under Loren, Pick's
going to ride high in the saddle again. We
see that now."

"What do you mean — again?"

"Nothing at all," Stub said hastily.

There was nothing for Ute to do but wait for Lake or Loren to show back since they could be off on any point of the compass. Ute watched the operation go on. The cattle looked good, and now, with the stampede a thing of history, were easy to work. The cutting was going faster, Ute saw.

Loren and Lake, who seemed to have become twins in recent weeks, rode in together. Both were affable and undisturbed at seeing Ute at the herd.

"Can't keep a good man down, eh, kid?" Loren said lightly. "Ready to start earning your beans again?"

"That's right." Ute looked at Lake, who only grinned at him.

"Why, that's fine," Lake said. "Good to see you around again. And I sure need a rest from this plague-taken job."

Having been so sure that a show of antagonism would come, Ute felt almost deflated. But, since he had twice come close to dying, he clung to his suspicions and his wariness. Those two had known that he would be back at the earliest possible moment. Apparently they had achieved what they wanted and were now willing to turn the reins back over to him.

"Where's the trail herd?" Ute said. "And who's keeping an eye on it?"

"Over on Clover Creek," Loren said. "A couple of the boys are camping there with it."

"Only a couple? You need half a dozen."

"Where you going to scare 'em up?" Loren retorted. "Anyhow, there's nothing there yet but the shoe-string stuff picked up on our grass."

"Pick's not holding on the Clover?"

"Not room enough. You know that."

Ute looked narrowly at Loren. "Pick's going to drive to the railroad with the rest, as usual?"

Loren shrugged. "I dunno, kid. It's like Joe claimed it would be. The shoe-stringers are getting mighty troublesome. It would be a good idea to show them they're in no position to sass Pick just because Tap's gone."

"I hear Joe keeps asking for sass," Ute said.

Lake scowled, but Loren spoke up for him, saying, "Joe's only tried to get it through their knotty heads that Pick still throws the big shadow in this country. But you're boss again. If you want to keep on coddling the bastards, you can."

"You got a lot of love for them, haven't you?"

"I don't have a bit." Loren started to walk

100

off, then turned back to say, "I almost forgot to tell you. I'm holding Olivia's stuff with mine."

"Olivia's — why?"

"I offered to and she accepted." Loren indulged himself in a thin smile, then, and left, Lake following.

For a moment afterward Ute scarcely drew a breath. He had known that Olivia was swamped just now, having had the full responsibility of Crosscut dropped so unexpectedly on her shoulders. He had offered to help her all he could, and it beat him why she had turned to Loren in the matter of getting her beef to the railroad. That hit him pretty hard, even if she had been honest in telling him which of the Taplan boys she considered the most competent.

As the day's work wound up and the tired punchers came in to camp, Ute saw that Stub Hines was not the only one who was glad to see him back on the job. Even some of Pick's own riders went out of their way to let him see their pleasure. Cheer seemed to rise up in the camp again, and the next morning work was resumed with a new heart that gratified Ute Taplan.

The round-up moved on up Horseshoe Basin. Ute could find nothing wrong in what had been done in his absence, nor in the way the work continued after his return. He had a natural, easy, yet authoritative way with the men. He got prompt, ungrudging obedience. And he was human enough to relish his awareness of how galling this was to Loren.

It was at the end of two weeks that Ginny showed up to rep because the gather was coming close to her own neighborhood. To Ute she seemed to be an entirely different girl, turned quiet and thoughtful. That was not like her at all. She stayed with the round-up through the next several days while her father's stuff was gathered and cut out. Then she dropped out of sight again. Ute didn't talk to her once during that time except about the work.

Yet he missed her afterward, and that was strange. Ever since finding himself so at odds with Olivia, his thoughts had been centered more than ever on her. She was a part of him, a person he depended on — or had. As he thought of this shift away from her to a strictly independent course of action, he recalled a statement Herb had made that he had considered downright ridiculous at the time. That he had found a sort of mother substitute in Olivia, even when she had been a button herself.

Now, having been around Ginny again

and having felt it wise to steer clear of her as much as possible, he was wondering why he never really felt for Olivia the hot, earthy impulses that rose in him at the very sight of Ginny. That was why they had never had any real understanding about being in love and wanting to get married. It struck him now that there was nothing progressive in their relationship. They had both been pretty contented with the way things stood. While with Ginny — well, a man couldn't be around her at any time at all without wanting more.

The day came when the big outfit made its final circle, branded its last calf and cut out its last steer to go on the market drive. Since leaving Pick's upper boundaries, the herd held on the Clover had grown much more rapidly than before. Little as he could spare the men, Ute kept a strong guard there. Actually he had no authority over that herd. When it trailed, a crew would be organized and a trail boss chosen.

But Ute was worried, even though the guards left with that stock never had anything alarming to report. The rustlers who supposedly had started the stampede seemed to have left the country. That, or they were waiting until the road herd had been built to its final size so that one big raid would do it all for them.

On the last night before the round-up crew broke up, Vic Rudeen rose to a stand at the campfire and called for attention. "It seems to me," he said, "that we might as well get set up for the railroad drive. Who's going to go, and who's going to boss it?"

"And put up the chuck-wagon?" Loren drawled. He had been rolling a cigarette at the fire and did not look up. He was the only Pick man on hand. The remark was so pointed that every man there looked startled and deeply embarrassed.

Ute frowned at Loren, wondering if he was trying to make it plain that Pick so far had been feeding the outfit — or if he had a deeper purpose in what seemed to be a completely uncalled-for question.

Rudeen's back had stiffened, and his cheeks turned red. He said, "None of the rest of us owns a chuck-wagon, Loren. Since the first steer bucketed past the first sage-bush, the big outfit in a locality has put up the chuck-wagon against the little feller's work. I put in ten times the work on Pick stuff that I did on my own. I figure that I earned my grub."

Loren lighted his smoke and tossed the match stick into the fire. "Have you shoe-stringers got the men to make up a trail crew?" he asked. "And still have anybody left to keep an eye on things at home? Have you got the horses it takes to make up a drive?" Callously he was pointing out the ways they had always been dependent on Pick.

Rudeen's face turned a deeper red. His eyes gleamed brighter in the flickering firelight. He said, "If Pick don't want its neighbors on its back, Loren, it had better come out and say so. Or are you just telling us to remember which side our bread's buttered on? So we'll put you or Lake in charge of the drive. We had all we can stomach of Lake on the round-up, man. Do you want to lead us to market?"

"Who'd you rather have, Vic?" Loren countered.

"Ute. Any day."

"Then why don't you go ahead and choose him."

Ute thought he saw what Loren was crowding for, at last. He had made his plain talk and now he wanted to see if they still had the courage to ignore him as they had in the first election.

"All right," Rudeen said promptly. "If you boys want to settle it, I'm putting up Ute. Even if we have to trail with a pack outfit — which we sure as hell can, Loren."

When nobody else spoke through a long, tension-fraught moment, Stub Hines said, "Move the nominations be closed." He was drowned out in an affirmative chorus.

Loren's eyes had turned colder, but he brought a grin to his lips. "You boys have elected your trail boss," he said and rose up.

"Pick's out, is it?" Rudeen said in an all but purring voice. He was angry enough now to brace Loren then and there.

"Pick and Crosscut," Loren said and then looked full at Ute. He tossed the cigarette into the fire and started toward the remuda.

Ute followed him. He caught up with Loren but waited until they were well beyond earshot of the camp to speak. "All along," he said finally, "Joe has riled those boys to get them sore enough to take the initiative in busting up with Pick. Why, man?"

"Don't you forget that I'm running Pick. I don't have to answer your questions. Or ask your advice. You've got a fair-sized herd to take to the railroad. Without a nickel's worth of your own beef in it, either. Short handed and short of horses. You better confine your worries to that and let me handle mine."

"We better have our showdown," Ute said dangerously. "I want to know how you account for marking up Tap's map, the way you did. Herb Latamore was your number one. He's dead. Out of the way, and it looks like you've been making more time with Olivia than you could have with him around. Hope to get her to entrust the ranch to you — or marry you and turn it over?"

"You're meddling again. That's Olivia's business and not yours."

"Well, what's your plans for the other basin ranches? You had them all on that list, except for Rocking A. You don't want that ranch because Pick ruined it a long time ago."

"Your horse sweat," Loren returned, "is something I don't have to listen to, either."

"You turn Pick into a range hog again, Loren, and I'll hound you to hell. I'm still a half owner, you know."

"Want to sell?"

"Can you raise the money?"

"I could."

"Then," Ute said, "Chance Donner's backing you in whatever you're up to. That's the only way you could buy me out — a loan from him."

"Donner knows you and me have been destined to bust up. But I asked a question. Do you want to sell out?"

"When I'm ready. And if you aim to try to

force me into it, you'll never get a deal."

Loren shrugged and went on toward the horse band.

EIGHT

As Ute approached the firelight again, he came upon a group of men who looked frankly glum and worried by what had transpired. With a sour glance at Ute, Rudeen said, "Loren sure put that one over on us, didn't he? All he wanted was a chance to break with us, and I sure set it up for him real pretty. Ute, you don't have to take the job we voted onto you. We know the kind of position it puts you in."

"I'm through with Pick," Ute said. "I have been ever since Tap died. If you're worried about Loren and figure he's set out to finish you, I agree. So I'll stick with the beef herd till you've sold it and made your payments to Chance Donner. I think that's what they're trying to prevent."

"How do you reach that conclusion, Ute?" Rudeen asked.

Ute fished into his pocket for the list of basin ranches he had taken off the map Loren had marked up for some secret purpose. He showed it to the others, saying, "For years Tap had a map of the Horseshoe.

I had reason to want a look at it, a while back. I found that Loren had numbered the different ranches. It puzzled me for a while. But finally I copied them off in numerical order. This list is surely a series that means something to Loren and Lake and likely to Chance Donner. We need to understand just what that is before we go any farther."

Rudeen examined the list, shook his head and said, "It don't mean anything to me, Ute."

"Just the same," Ute said, "Herb Latamore was number one and now he's dead. Loren's taken to courting Olivia and making a little headway, I guess. And that's something Herb would have objected to with the last breath in his body. Loren knew that full well. She's already starting to turn things over to him, whether she knows she's doing it or not. If he could get her to marry him, he'd have Crosscut lock, stock and barrel."

"Well, he sure can't marry all of us," Hines put in.

"More than one way to skin a cat," Rudeen said, "and Loren's a man who'd see all of them."

"I think Donner helped him work this list out," Ute said. "And I got a hunch that it shows your financial standing in the basin, which Donner knows well. Who's the most shaky and who's the best off. That would be the order in which they might be able to pick you off if they can get you cornered."

"Why, damn my hide," said old Tobie Jorgenson, who owned Pothook. "I come right after Crosscut on that list, and I'm sure as hell in a shaky financial condition. Got a mortgage payment on its second extension. Donner warned me a little while back that I got to pay up this fall or take the consequences. For the good of his stockholders, the man said."

Others, as they studied the list, nodded their heads. Talking it over, Ute's theory checked out right down the line — the order in which the ranchers enumerated judged themselves to be financially endangered.

"Then we've hit it," Ute said. "They've only got to shut off your income this one year and they'll finish some of you. Do it two years in a row, and they've got the whole basin."

Jorgenson said darkly, "Years back Tap Taplan and Chance Donner pulled about the same kind of stunt and got away with it. Pick pushed out over every spread around it, and Donner got his cut. Spreads that existed before your time, Ute. But they stopped when they'd gobbled up the first ring. Tap knew better than crowd his luck any farther. It looks like Loren feels more confident of himself, and that Chance Donner's got hungry again now that a new chance has come up."

Ute had heard so many unsuspected things against Tap and Pick in its early history that he took that one between the eyes without blinking. They were things, he knew, he would never have been told had he not renounced Pick and broken with Loren and encouraged the others in the basin to be more outspoken.

"What'll happen, then," said Rudeen, "is that we'll have trouble getting our herd to market. At best we picked ourselves a tough trailing job, and Loren broke with us so as not to have Pick stuff mixed in. We can eat out of a gunnysack, but it's going to take all the men and horses we can scrape together to get our steers to the stock pens. That means leaving our spreads short-handed or without anybody on 'em at all. If there's still rustlers around, they could make hay here while we're gone. Which could hurt as bad as losing the road herd would."

"Seems to me they'll concentrate on the road herd," Stub Hines said. "Top grade, all gathered, and where we'll get the cash if we're going to square up at the bank this fall. Boys, we've got to put that beef through no matter what happens at home."

Ute said, "Lake wouldn't call in the sheriff about the rustling. He and Loren made talk about us killing our own snakes. I think we ought to report it now, anyhow. If the sheriff comes looking around here, it would help to discourage dirty work here while we're off on the trail." The town of Starbow was not the county seat and seeing the sheriff meant a long ride to Red Buttes, which lay east of the Horseshoe. Thinking of that, he asked, "Stub, why don't you do that tomorrow while the rest of us move the herd off Pick onto somebody else's range?"

"I'll start at daylight," Stub agreed.

They put in the rest of that tension-filled evening trying to shape up their plans. But any way a man figured it, Ute realized, Pick had caught its little neighbors in the bight of the line that Loren and Lake had worked for from the start. It was at least better to have it all out in the open.

The whole next day was required to move the trail herd from Clover Creek onto Vic Rudeen's range. There were nearly two thousand head of cattle now, divided among nine small ranches. A drive of that size would require all of six riders, each puncher needing a saddle string of seven or eight.

They could pack their grub, equipment and bedding, and they could kill off any new-born calves. But let there be an attack somewhere in the rough country that had to be crossed, and the herd would be hard to protect.

Hines and Rudeen ran one-man outfits, an arrangement that was successful only when the basin pooled its round-ups and trail drives and loaned other work back and forth. Some other small operators had a few hired hands. To offset that, Ross Ide was crippled. Ginny could pinch-hit for him on the spread and even on a round-up, but Ute felt that it would be out of the question for her to go on the railroad drive. Ute himself would make a trail hand, and he was the only one of them without a ranch worth worrying about while he was gone.

With the herd moved, Ute told all but three men to get on home. Only one of the three left to guard the herd could sleep at a time. They staggered the watches, and Ute was at the cow camp when somebody hailed it from the distant darkness. He was on his feet at once. The low, natural rumble of the herd had kept him from hearing the approach, yet he realized that the visitor was friendly or he would not have declared himself before coming on in.

113

· There proved to be four men in the party that rode up to the camp, and they were all Pick punchers. They seemed uneasy, as if they did not know how they would be received, but were not hostile. At Ute's cautious nod they swung down.

Curly Jackson, a genial man who was one of Pick's top riders, grinned at Ute. "Man," he said, "us boys are on our way to the railroad. It struck us there might be a trail outfit we could latch onto and work our way."

"Aren't you going with Pick?" Ute asked, puzzled.

"Quit Pick this evening. We had all we want of that kind of guff, Ute. Need any men?"

Ute had to swallow. He said, "Why, thanks, boys. But we can't pay wages, and you know it."

"Who said anything about wages?" Curly demanded. "We collected our pay and we're lousy with money. We just want company to the railroad. Company of steers — and men we can like."

Ute had never felt so warm in the vicinity of his heart. They were all Pick's better men and had constituted a good quarter of its steady riding crew. They had come over voluntarily to help the little ranchers Pick so obviously was plotting against. Winter was due ahead, a time when riding jobs would be scarce as hen's teeth, but they were taking to the grubline rather than help Pick any longer.

"We can sure use you," Ute said. "You're foolish, but I'm damned if I don't love the lot of you."

Curly grinned at his companions — Slim Trawn, Bill Vainskeep and Dory Meadows. "Who said we were going to have a hard winter, boys? We're back to work, already. Ute, where do we begin?"

"It would help," Ute said, "if you'd take over this herd and guard it till we're ready to trail out. We've all got things to tend to before we roll our tails. The boys are throwing together a pack outfit and will pitch in to buy grub. We'll feed you and work you and maybe get you killed. But that's all I can guarantee."

"It's good enough," Curly answered.

Ute went to get his horse and tell the night herders that they could knock off and go home. To Vic Rudeen, he said, "You better tell Stub not to bother taking the long ride to see the sheriff, just yet. With Curly helping on the trail, enough of you can stay home to watch things here. And we'll wait till we've got something a lot more concrete before we call in the law."

He realized that he was taking a chance on the deserting Pick punchers. If Curly was lying about having really broken with Pick this was turning the herd over to Loren. Ute was willing to risk that on his judgment of the new men. He knew them all, and they were not cut out to be treacherous. The others backed him in that and showed considerable relief.

Then Ute struck out for Ross Ide's place, which lay beyond a low spur of distant hills and in against the malpais for he wanted to get an authorization from Ross to sell his steers at the railroad.

An hour later, when he drew near the little ranch house, he was glad to see lamplight through the windows. He called out as he rode in, a habit of the range country to put down apprehension. Ide, bent and supported by canes, stood in the doorway as Ute rode up to the porch steps.

"Well, howdy," Ide called. There was surprise in his voice. It was the first time Ute had paid this place a visit in a great while. "Anything wrong, Ute?"

"Not beyond what Ginny must have told you," Ute said, swinging down. He trailed reins and climbed to the porch, seeing Ginny now behind her father's stooped figure. It was some surprising when his pulse speeded up.

Ide stepped back, inviting Ute into the house. He had never been a large man and, bent over, he looked even smaller than Ginny. His painful handicap and the difficulties that stemmed from it had not taken the good humor from his face.

Ginny was in a dress again, with a ribbon in her hair and on her feet small slippers instead of riding boots. She looked cute as a kitten's ear rigged out that way, and it struck him that he had rarely seen her in anything but the rough working garb required by the nature of the country.

He took seat with them in the sitting room and told them what all had taken place since Ginny was last with the round-up. Ide's face darkened as he heard of Pick's open break with its little neighbors and how carefully it had been prepared.

"I took it for granted," Ute concluded, "that you'd want to trail your beef cut with us little fellows. Come over to get your authorization to sell it for you."

"Not necessary," Ginny said promptly. "We'll hold up our end, Ute. I'm going with you."

"Not by a damned sight," Ute retorted. "It's ten to one there'll be mean trouble."

"Don't argue, Ute. We'll take our share of the responsibility or we won't send anything along. Joe Lake fired me off the round-up, but you're not going to keep me out of that trail crew."

"This time it might be a finish fight."

"It's one I'd sure like to see finished."

"All right," Ute said, well aware that she could not be talked out of it. He rose to go, but the troubled abstraction of Ide's face bothered him. On impulse, he said, "Ross, I've got some startling opinions on it from oldtimers around here. Been wondering what a fairly recent newcomer — a man like yourself without so many of the oldtime grudges — would think about it. Did you ever form an opinion on whether I'm Tap's real son?"

Startled at first, Ide soon showed a look of relief. "I'm glad you asked, Ute," he said. "And I'll answer straight from the shoulder. Without knowing the history first hand, and just from knowing you three Taplans, I'd say that you ain't. You're cut from a different bolt of goods."

"I guess that ought to settle it."

"Why do you let it trouble you so?" Ginny said, then. "Believe me, Ute, I'd rather see you disprove your connection with that family than have you prove it. So would everyone else in the basin, excepting maybe Olivia."

Ute gave her a quick, hard stare. "Why do you say that?"

"You asked for unprejudiced views," Ginny said. "So I can't answer that one."

"I know why it keeps troubling him," Ide said to Ginny. "The fact that he might soon be in a shooting war against Loren. Ute, that's why I gave you my opinion that you weren't, ain't, and never will be a Taplan."

"For which same," breathed Ginny, "thank heaven."

"Loren's now showing the real stripe?" Ute asked.

Ide's eyes were sympathetic as he nodded. "Nobody would ever make the kind of talk to you that they would to me, since everybody knows how you worshipped old Tap. But from what I've heard, he never turned into the kind of benevolent despot you knew till he got along in years and had satisfied his appetites. It's hard to say where his lost kid really is, right now. But I'd bet my bottom dollar he's plotting for gain, the same as Loren is. I'm sorry, Ute. But you asked."

"Yeah. Thanks."

Ute did not show what he felt at that, for he was at least by training a Paiute Indian. He left after telling Ginny when the herd

119

was scheduled to trail out. She started to follow him outdoors, but changed her mind when Ide gave her a quick shake of the head. Ide knew that Ute wanted to be alone, just then. Ute was soon on his horse, going back to the cow camp.

Ide's talk had ripped away the last tatters of the veil that had been between him and the Taplan family, and Ute wished he was back among the people who had raised him. He had known love from them; he had given it to them. Never once had it been betrayed. Yet Tap had betrayed him, somehow — and so had Olivia.

Suddenly he knew what Ginny had started to say about Olivia. Slowly he began to realize that his hands were free. He had lived in a dream from which he was at last awakened. But it hurt. A man could not cut off so many years of his life without feeling and hating it plenty.

NINE

On the third morning thereafter the mix-branded herd hit the trail for the railroad, which lay six hard, day-long drives away, days of dust and heat, work and natural difficulties, and the almost certain experience of gun trouble somewhere along the way.

Moving with the remuda was a packstring that took the place of the usual wagons.

Yet the crew was in good spirits. The Pick punchers had made it possible for all but Hines, Rudeen and Ginny to remain behind and look out for the home ranches. Ute was glad they were so hopeful again, although he doubted that Loren would make his big strike in the basin and felt it was this road herd that would receive first attention.

For a time after leaving the Horseshoe, the market trail ran east. Thereafter it swung north past the foot of the mountains, only to turn back upon itself on the other side of the range. From there on the route meandered in the general direction of Sykes City. The mixed herd moved forward without trouble, breaking to the road, and there was no sign of Pick's having started out with its herd and Crosscut's. Loren had lost four of his best men in Curly and the others. He had to replace them, and Ute hoped he was having trouble doing it.

Ginny seemed to have turned back into a boy, covered with trail dust and working as hard as the others, so that a man took a close look before he realized she was a woman. She had a quiet faith in their ability to put the herd through to the loading pens, and this was partly responsible for the new

optimism in the men. Yet they all looked for
trouble and were constantly on guard.

They had made the big bend and were
moving back west again almost before they
realized it. But Ute did not consider this
particular stretch the logical place for
rustlers to make a try for the herd. The
farther away from the basin it happened,
the more innocent-appearing it would leave
Loren. Ute had two or three more dangerous places in mind, all yet ahead.

On the fourth day the mixed herd trailed
along the northern edge of the badlands.
Ute was wary, though even yet not expecting trouble. What now was a broken horizon
on the left was the vicinity he had supposed
Brig's gang might be using for headquarters.
They must have brought what steers they
had already rustled out through here. But
they would have dusted right on through,
for the spot was dry and almost without
grass.

The austere conditions, Ute realized,
would require the herd to make a poor, all
but dry overnight camp. He rode forward,
scouting for the best place to be found. He
had made this drive year after year and,
since they were ahead of Pick's herd, they
would have their choice of holding grounds
all along. He came to a piddling stream

called Lost Creek and saw that it had held up through the summer about as well as it ever did.

There was a big sage flat on the east side of the creek that would make as good a bedding ground as could be found. Although not satisfied, he swung back to meet the oncoming cattle. The herd's dust lifted heavily into the sky in the far distance. The lowering sun, due ahead now, troubled the steers and made them restless. But the riders kept them coming on in good formation.

Stub Hines and Ginny were riding point. When they came up, Ute waved an arm in the general direction of the distant sage flat and told them to head the herd off the trail. He fell in beside Ginny, a habit that was growing on him. This puzzled him a little, making him wonder if he was developing a new kind of dependence, and it made him a little cranky.

She wrinkled her nose as she looked about. "This the best we can do?" she asked, although it was not in a complaining way.

"What's wrong with it?" Ute asked, in mock surprise. "Sage, dirt and bare hills — what more do you want?"

Ginny pointed toward the adjoining badlands on the other side of the trail. "That's what's wrong with it."

Ute shook his head. "Those breaks run too far for us to pull away from tonight, Ginny. Anyhow, I feel safer here than I'll feel the rest of the way. There's been a lot of stuff run into those badlands from the Horseshoe side. I've seen the sign, myself. But it was run in there only so it could be brought out on this side and rushed out of the country. Reverse it and run something in from this side, and the only place it could come out would be back in the Horseshoe."

Ginny smiled at him. "I wouldn't dream of giving you an argument — but you're dead wrong. That rustling thing is hard to swallow. And the value of this herd is piddling compared with the real stakes in the game."

"Meaning?"

"That these steers don't have to be rustled. All that is necessary to break us is for them to be kept off the market."

"Just the same," Ute said stubbornly, "I think the strike will come farther along." Yet she had worried him more than he liked, so he added, "What would you do about it?"

"Drive all night and get past this rough country."

"Melting off a dollar's worth of fat from

every steer?"

"We might be able to afford that."

Ute only shook his head again. The point was swinging from the trail and coming smoothly to the creek and its scant water. He took satisfaction in the expert way it was being handled. Notwithstanding, it was a dangerously short-handed crew. He wished now that he had planned his start from the basin so as to pass well by here in the light of day.

Camp was set up by Lost Creek, with the herd drifted half a mile north where a rim would hold one side of it. The horse band was spotted between, horses usually being more alert to their surroundings than cattle and more apt to tip off the fact if other horses came near.

The sun dropped quickly beyond the hills to the west. The herd's dust soon cleared from the air. The scent of sage was pungent, and finally Ute began to ease up. He loved the outdoors, and he liked this scene of desperate men so coolly trying to work out their salvation.

The crew was too limited to afford a special cook and horse wrangler, the men taking turns in those jobs. That night it was Ginny who cooked supper, and though it was simple fare every man there swore it was the best he had ever eaten. In spite of the fact that she was no longer very feminine in appearance, Ginny was pleased. They helped her clean up the wreckage, afterward, and she was woman enough to let them do it for her.

Ute was obliged to keep four men on guard, each division of the crew taking half the night. He, Ginny, Curly and Stub were on the last watch. They turned in early, Ginny bedding down with the rest. But it did not much matter that there was no privacy for her. Nobody did more than pull off his hat and boots.

The broken nights of rest caused Ute to fall into a quick, heavy sleep. He did not awaken until his consciousness was invaded by the sudden heavy drum of hoofs. It brought him up in one springing motion, and he pulled on his boots standing up. The night was quiet except for the loping horse which, according to the swelling sound, was driving toward camp.

Then something else happened, a voice drawled out of the close night. "Lift your hands, man, and stand still!"

The sound came from behind Ute, from the cut-bank of the creek. For a second he nearly swung toward it. He knew already who was there. That was the lazy voice of the bantam, Brig. Ute knew enough about that man to realize he would be shot in the back unless he obeyed the command. With a soft and bitter curse at Brig, he shoved up his hands.

He knew that Brig was coming forward. But at that moment Stub lifted his head from the saddle he was using as a pillow, awakened and curious.

"Don't anybody start trouble," Brig warned and then came on into the camp. He had a .45 in his grip. He was alert to the oncoming horse and uneasy about it. The starlight showed the beard accumulated on his face, attesting that he had kept to the back country since his previous brush with Ute. He nodded toward the arriving rider and said, "That will be one of your boys, Ute. Don't try to warn him. I'll cover him when he comes up."

"Something slip on you, Brig?" Ute drawled.

"Not too bad."

Ute did not have to be told what was taking place. The nearly dry wash of Lost Creek had let Brig's men sneak up without being detected by the night guard. Brig had not wanted to risk a stampede by coming in shooting. For the same reason, the oncoming rider had fired no shots to call for help.

A beef scatter in this rough country would be as bad, almost, as an outright loss to rustlers.

By then Curly and Ginny had aroused from their sleep. The sight of Ute standing with a gun on him kept them from speaking or trying to raise up. But the oncomer was close, and suddenly Vic Rudeen's voice rolled ahead of him.

"Ute — something's haywire!"

He whipped up at the camp, then sat his saddle in frozen surprise. In an all-gone voice, he added, "Ain't that the truth?"

"Swing down, man," Brig said.

Rudeen obeyed. Now Brig ordered the others to their feet and bunched them. He was still listening for something, and Ute thought he knew what that was. His men were going to take the herd, and Brig wanted to hear it moving. Apparently he only meant to keep the camp immobilized while that happened.

"You could have picked yourself a better place," Ute said.

"Maybe," Brig admitted. "But in the best places, Ute, you'd have been more on the lookout."

The herd was only a vague mass out in the darkness. It began to show motion, Ute thought, and he was puzzled that the drift was this way when Brig could have saved time by cutting a long slant toward the forward trail. Unless — Ute went cold as he remembered what Ginny had said by implication. Loren had only to make sure this herd was lost to the basiners to profit from it greatly. Its intrinsic value was of little importance to him.

Ute stood there on the ragged edge of recklessness. He would rather see the herd scattered to hell and gone than in Brig's hands. He wished fervently that Ginny was not in the camp. He would risk his own hide in a try for Brig, as would Stub, Vic or Curly.

Ginny spoke up then in a voice charged with anger: "You don't make a convincing rustler. A killer, a half-pint of poison. But you'll never take the risk of getting this big a herd from here to some crooked market. You don't have that kind of nerve."

"Shut up," Brig said, but he sounded surprised.

Ignoring the command, Ginny pointed toward the malpais. "You'll scatter it in there. Your profit will come from Taplan and Donner. You're only trying to keep us from selling our beef."

"And you're plain loco," Brig retorted, but he was taken back.

Ute knew already that Ginny was right.

But it was all-fired important to Loren that it look like genuine cattle thieving. He wished that Ginny had not let that boil out of her. Brig might not consider it wise to leave behind him anybody who claimed that Loren was still his boss.

The cattle were definitely moving now. Ute could see riders at work with them. The remuda, not directly hazed, was scattering out but also picking up the drift of the cattle. Nothing lay ahead of them but the badlands. Drifted into them deeply and there scattered, they would be doomed. There was not enough forage or water in the malpais, that he knew of, to support a herd like this any time at all. To flush the cattle out again would require a bigger force of men than the basin's little outfits could muster for any extended period. It would require more time than remained until winter had closed in.

Ute just wasn't going to stand for that. Yelling, "Vic — get aboard and bust up that point!" he drove himself full at Brig.

He didn't expect to live through it, hoped only to give Vic a chance to get away. He made a side thrust, a swerve as he shoved ahead. Brig fired without hesitation. The impact of the bullet knocked Ute back on the other tack. But before Brig could shoot again, Curly had hit him in a headlong dive. Curly came in fast, hard, a battering ram. Ute's will broke then, and he went down. But he got right up.

Stub yelled, "Come on, Ginny!" as Vic went up to the saddle. Brig's shot had warned his raiders that something had gone wrong. Vic drove his horse straight at the oncoming herd. Stub and Ginny sped toward the horses kept on picket at the camp.

Ute's whole side was numb, but he could still move. Curly and Brig still fought on the ground, Curly trying to get Brig's gun. Ute swept down and caught Brig's hand, nearly breaking it when he wrenched the piece loose. Then he stood back, panting, hardly able to keep himself up.

"Got him covered, Curly," he gasped. "Hit leather."

Curly broke free and climbed to his feet. Without a word, he raced out to get aboard his own horse.

Brig did not try to rise from the ground. Ute knew that he, himself, would have trouble sticking a saddle, so he stood there with the gun aimed at Brig. It wouldn't have taken much to cause him to pull the trigger. Out in the distance horses were running upon the herd, through the remuda that preceded it, the riders shouting and shooting as they sped along.

There was only an outside chance that they could do any good. Cattle, when startled by something due ahead, would sometimes cut a maneuver a cowhand called bulling back. Ute's riders were trying to cause the herd to reverse its direction, thus keeping it out of the badlands.

Ute found himself incapable of leaving the dangerous try to them alone. In savage anger, he bent and put the gun barrel across Brig's head. The man threw up a protecting hand but caught most of the blow on his skull and went limp. Ute didn't have time to tie him up so he hit him again with the gun barrel. One horse remained on picket. He headed for it in a weaving run.

He had all he could do to pull up into the saddle, but his side was still too numb to cause him much pain. By then Brig's men were firing all along the flanks of the herd and at its rear, trying to offset the effort to bull back the herd. They were cutting it, for the herd came on. As he drove his horse forward at a neck-risking speed, Ute saw it coming on at a trot that would soon be a gallop, then a headlong, unmanageable run. Ute's four riders had been forced to break off and whip out into the clear at the last possible moment. They were on the flanks, then, shooting at the outlaws, trying to drive them away from the cattle.

Ute cut a lefthand quarter, then the first steers swept past him, the dust of their hoofs boiling up to obscure the whole scene. Gunfire rattled far ahead of him, and he could hear it from across the herd. Now and then a stitch of pain hit his wound. His shirt was soaked with blood, which he could feel trickling down his leg. But he thought that a rib had deflected the bullet, the catch indicating that the rib had been broken.

He had not forgotten Ginny, who was a steady worry on the edge of his mind. She had been wearing a gun on the drive and doubtless was using it now. Then a horse came thundering toward him. It had a white face, which told him that it carried an enemy. In the next instant a gun flashed on its back. Ute flung one grim shot. The horse kept on, but its rider left the saddle. Then three more men swept past, shooting as they rode.

Targets were tricky, hard to make out in the dusty confusion. Ute emptied the gun he had taken from Brig. Thereafter he had to swing outward as the broadening mass of the herd swept in. Now and then a horseman streaked along with the running cattle. Ute knew it was a hopeless proposition, then. The steers were not yet in full, stampeding flight. Enough of Brig's men had passed on ahead to keep them pointed straight toward the badlands. Ute could only maintain his precarious saddle seat and wait.

No more men swept past him. At last he saw the frayed drag of the herd. Again he waited, dreading an accounting of his courageous but badly outnumbered crew. He thought of Brig, then, who was back at the camp. He wanted that man. Turning his horse, he headed on an angle that ran toward the place. No horse had been left there, and this was poor country for a man to tackle in high-heeled boots. But if Brig had come to, he would prefer walking to waiting there. Again Ute drove in his spurs.

TEN

He let out a sigh of relief when he saw that Brig was still out cold on the ground. The county had a fair enough sheriff. After what Ute would charge, the officer could set to sweating Brig for all he was worth. Ute went to the packing equipment, found rope and tied Brig up.

He had just finished when he heard horses coming in from the now empty sage flat. In spite of the disaster, he felt relieved when he could count four of them. As far as they knew, Ute had not left the camp. He was standing in a weary slump when they rode in.

In a roughened voice, he called, "See anything of the other boys?"

"They're all right," Curly answered. "But they ain't got horses. Don't know where they'll get any, seeing that our remuda went with the herd. Ute, I don't see how you stayed alive. That polecat shot pointblank."

"A foolish thing, Ute," Ginny said, a strangely soft quality in her voice. "But so like you. And, if you want to know, so unlike a Taplan."

"Hell," Ute retorted, "there was nothing brave about it. If Brig had kept the upper hand, he might have shut your mouth for good. You sure gave off head."

"Let's see what damage he did to you," Ginny said woriedly and she stepped down from the saddle.

He let Ginny and Curly dress the wound, which was an angry gash running along a rib halfway up his side. The rib was cracked, he knew from the pain, but he had got off easier than he had had a right to expect.

Stub Hines took a look at the man on the ground and said, "Well, we swapped two thousand head of steers for a cross between a lobo and a coyote. Poor trade, I call it."

"He's worth something," Ginny answered. "If we can tie him to Loren we can get damages from Pick and stop Loren dead in his tracks."

"That's our only hope," Vic Rudeen commented. "If Brig's men do a good job of scattering our stuff in the breaks, we'll be months rounding up what manages to stay alive. At best, it would be too late to drive to the railroad." His voice was low, metallic with discouragement.

"Unless we can do some good with Brig," Ute admitted, "Loren's got it made." He was already seeing what he had to do now, himself, although he was not ready to disclose the plan to the others. He had to see Donner at once. "And when those lobos miss Brig they're liable to come back after him. We've got to watch out."

Presently the three missing men trudged in on foot — Slim, Bill and Dory. They were unhurt. They had been surprised, one by one, then taken out and set afoot too far away from the herd to interfere with the outlaws. Vic Rudeen explained that he had been warned when, making a circle of the herd, he had seen horses standing with empty saddles off in the distance. Instead of going on to where he might run into trouble, himself, he had whipped back to arouse the camp.

Ute said, "Well, that's the end of the trail drive, and I'm out of a job. But I suggest, Stub, that you and Vic put Brig on a horse and take him to the sheriff right now. Watch yourselves all the way. Curly, you and the rest of the boys are nailed down here till Ginny and me can go back to the basin and send you horses."

"Too far to walk," Curly agreed.

Although the man was not eager to disclose the fact, it became evident that Brig had recovered consciousness. Ute did not try to sweat him — that had become a job for the sheriff. When daylight came, the forlorn party cooked a meal. Thereafter Hines and Rudeen started off with Brig as their prisoner. Ute and Ginny left at once for their crestfallen return to Horseshoe Basin.

Although it had taken much longer with the cattle, they covered the distance that same day. They went at once to Ross Ide's, where Ginny insisted on Ute's laying over to eat and rest. Ide received the bad news with a distinct shock on his face. A cowman worked through an entire year for the sake of the fall market drive. But Ide did not mention the worries that must have crowded into his mind.

The Ide house was small, and when Ute had eaten supper he slept in the hay in the barn. He rose at dawn, refreshened but with his feeling of guilt undiminished and with his wounded side still hurting him like fury. He could dismiss the pain with the stoicism his childhood among the Paiutes had given him. But the feeling of personal responsibility for what had happened could not so easily be thrust aside. Excuses did not matter to him. He had failed in his undertaking, and now a whole basin faced ruin.

He went up to the house. Ginny was already out of bed, cooking breakfast, and Ute had decided that it might be smart to get her view on a few things, seeing how much shrewder she had been in reading the situation at the Lost Creek camp the day they reached there. He spoke to her through the open kitchen door but stopped on the porch to wash his sleep-hot face and comb his hair. Then he stepped into the kitchen.

After her disheveled appearance on the trail, it gave him a pleasant surprise to inspect her neat hair, her fresh face and dress. Her vitality had always been amazing and now one short night of sleep seemed to have washed weariness and trouble out of her. But she was graver than the old Ginny, as she had been ever since the start of Loren's aggression.

She nodded at the table and said, "Sit down, Ute. I've got hot cakes in the warming oven."

He took seat, trying to remember how long it had been since he had eaten a meal in her house. He said, "Ginny, I'm going to buy every steer that was in the herd."

She turned swiftly, holding a platter of griddle cakes and bacon in her hands. "Do what?" she gasped.

He had to laugh at her complete amazement. "You mean to say *with* what, I reckon. Ginny, Loren offered to buy me out, and I'm going to sell. That way we can be sure of damages from Pick without relying on the law at all."

Ginny sat down, her bewilderment causing her to hold onto the platter instead of putting it on the table. "Are you doing that just to help us or to beat Loren?"

"Both. And if you can let go of those hot cakes, I'm hungry."

She put the platter on the table, then, and blew out her cheeks. She rose and went to the kitchen range and poured two cups of coffee. She forgot them, returned empty-handed, and sat down again.

"You've got me beat," she said. "But I wish Loren had heard you say that. And I wish that Tap had, too. You've proved yourself, Ute. Right out of that snake-blooded family. But if Loren suspects what you'll do with the money, you'll never get a deal through."

"That's the rub," Ute admitted. "I thought about it a lot last night. I'm going to make my offer to Donner. I think he'd jump at a chance to buy half of Pick at the price I'll make him. Then I'm going to deposit the money for the lost steers in the basiners' accounts. Get it done and have a receipt before he sees through it."

"Neat, Ute," Ginny said. "But you've completely overlooked an important angle. We won't let you do that. It would be downright charity."

"Just damages from Pick," Ute insisted. "Ginny, I don't want any part of that ranch now that I know how Tap built it up. It's too late to compensate most of the men he hurt. But I can make amends for Loren, and if Donner gets in with him Loren's going to have his hands full just holding on to his own share."

"Ute, that's so like you I could cry."

"Cut it out," he said, half angry. "I haven't told you all of it. If I buy those steers, they're mine and I could use them. I don't have a thing to run on Rocking A. If having Brig in our hands has stopped Loren from interfering, there's a chance the basiners can flush out a good part of that herd. What's so soft-headed about that?"

"You don't like to be called soft-headed?"

"No. Reminds me of what a certain somebody once said."

"Olivia?" Ginny laughed, then, and quickly added, "Don't answer that. Men are like eggs, I guess. Olivia likes hers hard. Me, I don't mind if mine are a little soft."

Ross Ide's pain kept him from sleeping well, and he was late in hobbling into the kitchen. Arriving at that moment, he gave no sign of having heard what was being said. He still looked drawn and uneasy, and he went on outside.

Ginny reached across the table and dropped a brown hand on Ute's arm. In a half-whisper, she said, "Whoever your family was, Ute, they were fine people. You've proved that. Don't ever doubt it again, and be proud of your background. Because I am. So very proud."

Except for the fall of Ide's boots on the porch, then, Ute would have gone around the table after her. For no other reason than the warmth of affection in her lively brown

141

eyes. Some day he was apt to forget himself and take advantage of the gate in her he thought he knew how to open.

When Ide came back into the kitchen, Ute said, "Ross, have you got any blank checks on Donner's bank?"

"Blanks is all I got," Ide said.

"I'd like the loan of a handful."

"What's that?" Ide asked in sharpened interest.

"Private business for a while, Ross," Ute said and smiled at the man. "Just let me have the blanks."

Although puzzled, Ide looked at Ginny and said, "You know where they are, Ginny. Get them for him."

Ginny motioned Ute into the next room. There was a more formal dining table in there. She got him some check blanks, then set out pen and ink for him. Ute went to work.

As trail boss, he had known the tally of each owner in the lost herd. He also knew the market value of the steers at the railroad. He did his figuring, then began to write checks. Since there was no chance of getting the necessary endorsements for deposit in time, he made them out to cash. If he succeeded in what he wanted to do, he would endorse them to the basiners' separate accounts.

Finished, he put the checks in his shirt pocket and carefully buttoned down the tab. He went out to the kitchen, where Ginny now sat while her father ate his breakfast, and said, "Ginny, I don't want you trying to take horses back to Curly and the boys. You go over to Pothook and tell old Jorgenson about it. He can rescue Curly's bunch. I'm going to Starbow first, then back to Rocking A. Be two or three days before Stub and Vic get back. You organize a meeting at my place for Friday evening, will you?"

Ginny started to speak, but since he did not again mention his intention of selling his share of Pick, she kept silent about that plan. She agreed to his suggestion about the horses, promised to have everybody at Rocking A the night he wanted, and to be there herself whether he wanted that or not.

"And you see a doctor while you're in town," she added. "I might not have put you back together right."

She did not follow him outdoors, and he went to the corral and caught his horse. The chore gave him trouble, reminding him of the useless days he had spent when his shoulder was hurt. But this time he could still operate, and he was mighty glad of that. The time for the big showdown, he felt, was

143

right at hand.

He was soon on the long trail to town. He still wore a bloody shirt and the stubble of beard he had accumulated on the trail. But that was the way he wanted to present himself to Chance Donner. Because he found that he could not stand hard riding, he did not reach Starbow until around noon. His side was aching like fury by then, even so, but he put off seeing the doctor until he had done his business at the bank.

He racked his horse before that brick structure and entered the place at once. The clerks were busy with customers from other parts of the country, none of whom Ute knew very well. He went directly on to Donner's door, which stood open, and walked right in without invitation.

Chance Donner was at work on something that lay on his desk. He looked up with a frown at the intrusion, but the protest that he had meant to voice died in his throat. Then, "I thought you were on the trail, Ute. What happened? Who shot you?"

Ute glanced down at the blood on his shirt. He said, "Maybe it was just the mosquitoes down around the deltas on Rocking A. Donner, I'm going to need more money than I ever figured on out there. I split clean with Loren, as you probably know. I don't want any part of Pick again. I won't dicker with Loren, but it struck me you might like to buy me out. If not, he's interested. He asked me a while back if I wanted to sell."

Donner put down his pen and leaned back in his chair. He kept staring at Ute. He wet his lips, then said, "Are you serious?"

"I wouldn't come here for any social visit, Chance. You know that. And knowing Tap's business and Loren's, you know what Pick's worth better than I could ever find out. What would you say would be a fair price for my half interest?"

"Fifty thousand." Donner said readily. It was too quick and too round a figure to be a fair one, Ute realized. "Somewhere around there, Ute."

"Would you pay that much for it?" Ute asked, rounding his eyes a little as if he had been pleasantly surprised. "I mean today — right now."

"Why," Donner said, "it ought to be inventoried and all that. But I got a habit of keeping a pretty close eye on Pick. When Tap wanted to know something, he wanted the answer right now. But I'd say fifty thousand looked reasonable, Ute, give a little, take a little, maybe."

"Would you pay it?"

145

"You're set on it?" Donner stroked his jaw. "It could only be a contract of sale, just yet, pending the time when Tap's estate is finally settled. But it would be as good as a sale. One I don't think Loren could get set aside, although he might try." The man was heated, all right, by the prospect of getting any kind of a grip on Pick.

"Just fix up the papers," Ute said. "I've got to go to the doctor. Be back in an hour. Is that time enough?"

"Plenty," Donner said and for the first time he let a glint of satisfaction show in his eyes.

Easy as taking land away from an Indian, Ute thought.

Then, a little caution showing in his voice, Donner said, "How do you want the money?"

"Credit it to my account," Ute said, "and give me a deposit receipt." He walked out before the man could let unsatisfied curiosities dim his aroused appetite for gain. Privately, he was as gratified as Donner was by the deal.

The doctor happened to be in his office, which was in the lodge hall building. Ute had to wait his turn but, since he had to kill time anyway, he did not mind that. Presently the doctor was looking at his wound, manipulating the hurt rib and listening with a stethoscope for what he called *crepitus.*

Finally the medico shook his head, saying, "I don't know what they make you cowpokes out of. The bone's cracked, but that's all. I'll strap you up, and you can go get into more trouble."

Ute let himself be bandaged from his armpits to his belt line, and the doctor made it too tight for real comfort. Yet he found that the support stopped the hurting in his side. The thing took a while, and when Ute emerged onto the street again he had not long to wait until it was time to go back to the bank.

This time Donner was watching and waiting for him, waving him right on in. The banker had a sheaf of papers on the desk. Under more leisurely circumstances, Ute would have felt it advisable to have a lawyer handle a deal as big as this one. But he did look the papers over closely before he signed a thing. The forms were printed and were not apt to be tricky. The parts that Donner had filled in with a pen seemed to be in order. Donner even had a deposit slip there that credited the money to Ute's checking account. He pushed the slip over indifferently, and just as casually Ute picked it up and put it in his pocket. Then, taking the pen, Ute signed away his half of Pick without regret.

The two clerks witnessed the signatures. When that was done, Ute looked at one of them and said, "By the way, I got some checks to deposit for some neighbors of mine. Didn't give me their pass books. So just write me receipts."

Donner's mouth had sagged open. He said, "What neighbors, Ute?"

"Why," said Ute, "the men I went on the trail drive with. I've got their beef checks."

"Beef checks? Are you crazy — ?" Donner broke off. He had betrayed himself and was caught. He could not say that he knew the little ranchers in the Horseshoe had received no beef checks, had little chance of doing so in the regular way.

He had not had time to learn what had happened on the trail, but he must have known of the plan. Ute's wound and early return to the basin had told him that the plan had been carried out. For a moment there was a look of protest, of mounting anger in the man's eyes. He knew that he had been tricked but could not do a thing about it at the moment.

Anxious to get the deal put through the way he wanted, Ute seized the arm of the teller and towed him out to the lobby. He made his deposits, getting the receipts he demanded.

Before he left the bank, he paused in Donner's doorway again. The man sat motionless at his desk, staring straight ahead. Ute said, "It might interest you, Donner, to know that the sheriff will be poking around here pretty soon. About a road herd that was jumped on Lost Creek and run into the malpais. It's hard to tell what all he'll look into here. The transactions I just made had all better show up real plain in your books in case he comes in here about it."

"You get the hell out of here," Donner snapped.

Back on the street again, Ute thought of several things that he had to do before he left town. He had plenty of money left, after buying the cattle, with which to do them. He meant for it to do what he had described to Ginny, to make restitution of the gains Pick had made at the expense of others, as far as he could accomplish that. First he went to the feed store and arranged for concentrates to be hauled out to Rocking A. The grass out there was poor but had not been grazed and would do part of the winter feeding. Ute bought enough extra feed to run through the whole winter, an expense he would not have had except for

Pick and which Pick could now stand. The feed man agreed to get somebody to start hauling to Rocking A at once. Ute wrote him a check.

Next he went to a mercantile where he placed a big order that included blasting supplies and tools, and there he wrote another check. It gave him a grim satisfaction to be drawing on Pick without Loren's knowledge and regretted that he would not be able to see his face when Loren found out about it.

The tight bandage that the doctor had put on him made the ride home easier for Ute. He had a sense of triumph in the way he had managed to check Loren's carefully planned coup. But he fully understood that this gain was only a temporary one. The men he was up against were merciless and clever.

Twilight came in, followed by the first darkening sweep of the night that caught him well short of Rocking A. He was not altogether easy as he rode on, after that. All the while there had been a worry in the back of his mind, and with the night it came in closer. By telling Donner that the sheriff was coming in to investigate the situation in the basin, he had hoped to discourage the banker from trying to reverse the deal through crooked bookwork at the bank.

As long as the receipts in Ute's pocket were outstanding, Donner was not apt to try anything of that nature. But if Donner could recover the receipts, he might in his desperation attempt to deny the whole transaction, especially the deposits that had been made on the behalf of the ranchers whose spreads he coveted. Cold began to seep into Ute in spite of the warmth of the night. The triumph was suddenly gone, and harsh realities again pressed against him. Horseshoe was locked in a fight to the death, and only another phase of that fight had been concluded.

ELEVEN

Although he arrived safely at Rocking A's benighted buildings, it was something less than an elating experience for Ute. The deep melancholy of the deserted old place stood out. He had watered his horse at the creek crossing, but the tired animal was also hungry, and there was nothing on hand in the musty old barn with which to feed it but a litter of lifeless, dusty hay. When he had unsaddled, Ute turned the animal out into the horse pasture so it could graze, which left him without a mount at hand.

He had no bedding for himself except the sweaty saddle blanket, which he took to the cabin. The bunk, built against a wall, still held straw. He was asleep within minutes after he had stretched out there.

Up early the next morning, he cooked breakfast over an open fire from food he had brought out from Starbow in a gunnysack. His next chore was to make the place livable, although he would have little to work with until a wagon came out from town with the rest of what he had bought. Yet he would have to clean the well before he could use it, and the water he would draw out could well be put to scrubbing the shacklike cabin. After the meal, he got busy.

Before he realized it, the sun stood at high noon. By then he had cleaned the litter from the cabin and yard, knocked down the cobwebs and washed the few windows. A cool breeze riffled across the little bowl that was to be his headquarters site. It freshened the place so that, together with the cleaning, the atmosphere was much more inviting. He fixed himself another meal and was on the point of attacking the stagnant old well when he espied horses coming in on the town trail.

He felt an instant bolt of alarm, although he had hidden the bank receipts that were a deep worry to him. Then the feeling changed nature and he grinned in recognition. It was Curly Jackson and the three Pick punchers who were associated with him. They were on Pothook horses, he saw as they came nearer. Ginny had carried out her chore, and they must have ridden hard to get here this soon. All four newcomers wore grins as they rode in.

Curly pushed back his hat and said, "Well, man, this is the second time lately I've hit you up for a job. You need a crew on this new spread of yours?"

"What I need first," Ute said, "is a herd for a crew to work at."

"All right," said Curly, "we'll rustle you a herd."

"By damn," Ute said on a slow intake of breath, "maybe you could, Curly, at that. I sold my half of Pick yesterday. The owners don't know it yet, but I bought the trail herd we lost. If you boys want to buscow them steers out of the malpais for me, you've got a job. It's a situation that won't keep, and I'll pay top wages."

"Hired yourself some good men," Curly said. "When do we eat?"

Excitement had leaped into Ute. This was a lucky break, and he had need of one. The sooner he could get a crew into the malpais, the better would be the chances of flushing a good part of that herd out of there.

While the men fixed themselves a meal at his invitation, Ute explained in detail what he had done since he last saw them.

When he had finished, Curly said, "Many a time I heard Loren Taplan call you an Injun. If he's a white man, then I wish I could change my color."

They talked over the proposed work. Ute gave Curly a free hand to go into the malpais on his behalf and get out what cattle he could find. He would outfit them as soon as the wagon came from town. But the large number of horses required for such an undertaking presented a problem harder to solve. The little ranches had been cleaned out of them by the remuda that was captured with the herd. Buying more on the market would take too long a time. But Curly was hopeful of picking up the mounts they needed from the escaped horse band, itself. He knew some of the water holes in the malpais and where grass would be to draw the animals and hold them.

The newcomers had ridden all night, and when the plans were well shaped, they stretched out in the shade to catch up on sleep. Ute went on with the work of cleaning the well, his spirits greatly lifted again. Time after time he had beaten Loren in a simple contest of popularity. That was now worth more to him than any part of Pick or the Taplan name. Curly's persistent siding of the little ranchers was going to make a big difference again.

Ute had barely finished cleaning the well when a Starbow teamster pulled in. The arrival awakened Rocking A's new crew, which set to work helping to unload the wagon. They worked into the evening, getting the new stove set up and everything else placed where it belonged. Now they had coal-oil lamps and lanterns to light when darkness rolled in. The place looked like something, finally. To Ute it already seemed like home.

The teamster stayed for the night, starting back for Starbow the next morning. The others set to work, making up a camp outfit to take into the malpais. At noon Curly rode out with his men, all of them feeling confident.

"You're a going concern," Curly said in parting. "You stay and get set. Before you know it, steers will be boiling out of the badlands for you to worry over."

"And you keep your eye peeled," Ute warned. "With Brig gone and it being probable that the sheriff will be in there beating the canyons, it seems likely that the rest of that gang has drifted by now. But don't take that for granted. Neither Loren nor Donner is a man to quit easy. We've got to figure on a run for our money."

"They'll get as good as they give," Curly said. He sounded cocky, but Ute knew he was plenty capable of making good on that. Curly was the type of puncher who could ride onto any spread of his choice, ask for a job and get it.

They had taken Ute's one horse to pack on, leaving him afoot. But their first effort would be to recover some of the thirty-odd range horses now scattered in the depths of the badlands. If they had luck, Curly was going to bring Ute a couple of saddlers and take back a bigger supply of provisions to set up his camp.

Ute had another day to wait before the basiners would come for the meeting he had asked Ginny to arrange. He had nothing as yet to indicate whether Stub Hines and Vic Rudeen had got back after turning Brig over to the sheriff. They had had the time, and Ute figured that they would get in touch with him immediately to report what the sheriff planned to do.

Lacking a horse, Ute could only go on

with the repairs at Rocking A headquarters. He also could get ready for the substantial number of steers he now hoped to recover from the badlands. He had range, with a feed supplement already ordered, but there remained the more pressing matter of water supply. He was ready to tackle that now and could do it even without a horse, for the wherewithal had come out from Starbow on the wagon.

Now that there was danger of his being watched closely by Loren, he knew that he had to make his try for water at night, and preferably in the night just ahead. It was not too far to walk to the deltas, carrying the dynamite. He decided to start the effort as soon as it was dark enough for him to work without too great a chance of being detected.

He had gone to the house and was fixing supper when he heard a rider coming on at a hard pound. The situation had grown so deadly that he could no longer take a thing like that in ease. He swung out into the ranchyard to perceive that the rider was a girl. A moment later he had recognized Olivia. Ginny often rode like a wild wind, but it took urgency to make Olivia crowd a horse that way. He felt his throat draw tight as he watched her come in.

157

"What's wrong, Olivia?" he yelled at her.

She reined up the horse and slid from the saddle, pushing back her windswept hair. She said, "I've got bad news for you, Ute." Her tight face showed that it was almost too much for her to bear.

"You all right?" he asked.

"It's not me. But Stub Hines and Vic Rudeen. Joe Lake sent back word to Loren. Loren thought you ought to know but didn't want to talk to you, himself. He came over and asked me to do it."

In a drawn voice, he said, "What happened to them, Olivia?"

"They're dead, Ute. Pick trailed Monday. They found those two a few miles the other side of Lost Creek. Both had been shot to death and left there. Lake said it looked like a clean-cut ambush."

There was a moment in which Ute seemed to have no physical body at all. At last he found the voice to say, "Just the two of them there? There wasn't anybody else around?"

"That's all Joe said. Who else would there have been?"

"A man," Ute said, "that they were taking to the sheriff. The one that led the wild bunch that scattered our herd into the badlands. His cronies took him away from Stub and Vic and murdered them. Did Lake

158

report it to the sheriff?"

She nodded, adding, "I heard about your herd, Ute. I was sorry to hear what had happened."

"You showed good sense in turning your beef cut over to Loren."

"Ute, I've wanted to explain that. He just offered to take care of it for me. Right now I feel swamped, with Dad going so unexpectedly and everything falling onto my own shoulders. I welcomed the chance to have him take care of that one worry."

He saw that she had no suspicions of Loren, the way Ginny had felt them intuitively from the start. Olivia had known her father's uneasiness about the new set-up at Pick and apparently had shared it at the start. But she had changed a lot, now that she was on her own. Ute still was not going to set her straight about Loren. The rest of the basin had picked sides in the conflict between the brothers on the basis of character appraisal, alone. Let Olivia do that, too, or let developments open her eyes for her.

Looking down at her concerned face, he knew that this moment was different from any other they had shared. He had a sense of her having failed him, for the first time and at a time when he would least have expected it. No matter what lay between

159

them in the future, if he was to have one at all, he would never be able to forget that failure completely. Not when another woman had supported him right down the line.

Olivia seemed to sense the change herself. Maybe she had been aware of it much longer than he had. She saw that her account of why she had thrown in with Pick for the drive had explained nothing to him. Yet oddly she seemed to feel no wish to try again. A defensive resolve grew on her face, which changed again into the irritation she had shown him since the start of the trouble.

She said, "Loren told me that you've signed over your interest in Pick to Chance Donner."

"Anything wrong with that?"

"Maybe not. But why did you consider it your responsibility to pay for the steers that were lost? Just because you were trail boss?"

He nearly told her why, then, but caught himself before he had done it. Roughly he said, "And that is wrong?"

"Misguided and foolish. You didn't owe them that much, Ute, if you owed them anything at all. But it's your affair, I guess." Nodding then and giving him only the lesser part of a smile, she rose back to the saddle and was gone. He watched until she had

160

receded into the distance, the ground swells and sage swallowing her.

But his numbed mind went back then to Stub Hines and Vic Rudeen. Without knowing it, Olivia had brought information of two cold-blooded murders that Ute knew had to be laid at Loren's door. Yet, whether or not she realized it, she was moving closer to the man all the time. He saw at once Loren's motive in telling her of the so-called foolishness of selling the half interest in Pick and using the proceeds to help a bunch of greasysackers. That proved the incompetence of Tap's Indian ward, and it seemed to have had the effect on Olivia that Loren had wanted.

But he had not long to brood about her. He felt a natural grief for Stub and Vic, for they had become his close friends. There was a portent in their deaths, also. They had never got to the sheriff with Brig and a report of the jumped trail herd. Instead Lake had sent word to the law officer of their bodies having been found. He and Loren would have their own story to tell about that discovery. Brig and his wild bunch were probably back in action, a fact of which Curly Jackson should be warned.

Now Ute cursed the fact that he was still without a saddle horse. And the meal he had started for himself got no further along. He sat in the kitchen through the gathering night. Sometimes he thought about Olivia and the hardness that had come up in her so unexpectedly. But his thoughts always returned to his dead friends. Two spreads in the basin had been vacated by those deaths.

Loren had not foreseen the chance to accomplish that, but he had not expected so much opposition from his own supposed brother, either. It looked like he had torn up his original schedule and was taking advantage of every opportunity that came along.

When night was full upon the range, Ute stirred from his apathy. He had a job to do at the deltas, and now he needed something badly to occupy his mind. He got a new shovel that he had had sent out from town. He placed a dozen sticks of dynamite in a gunnysack, together with a box of caps and a coil of fuse. Thereafter, he struck out for the creek, a distance of half a mile from the cabin.

The steady swing of his long-gaited walk was soothing to his nerves. The stars were out, but their light was so dim that he was not much worried about being seen at what he meant to do. It seemed no time at all until he reached his destination, the choked mouth of what he now knew to be the original main channel of the split creek.

The cloggage, he had determined on his previous visit, had settled and impacted and become mainly overgrown with brush and weeds. He had explosive enough for two charges, which he thought would be required to open it up at the present water stage. It would be a job, even without the handicap of his lameness.

He selected his first location with great care, and it took a long while to dig down into the sand, gravel and silt far enough to set half the dynamite. He used a long fuse and afterward, afraid that the earth would simply blow out at the top, he carried rock from the old creek bed to pile on the fresh digging.

Sweat streamed from him. His whole hurt side ached steadily, and he was dead tired even by the time he had finished the first loading. But he knew that he would get only this one chance, so he moved to his second marked spot and started the labor all over again. He was racing against daybreak before he was done. But with the work's completion, his fatigue seemed to leave him suddenly, and even the gnawing pain in his side grew less noticeable.

He had taken his matches from his pocket

to keep them from being soaked with his sweat. He got a match and struck it and held it to the first fuse. When that was sputtering, he wheeled and bolted for the other charge. He had barely made it on to the cover of the nearby brush when the first blast went off, a muffled but swelling boom. He swung about and through the bright starlight saw earth leap into the sky. That was followed by a rain of loose dirt and rock that came down about him.

Then the second charge let go. It shot with the same clean effect. In spite of his grief and trouble, Ute grinned as he watched from a safe distance. Then he went in to inspect his work and found the muddy water let in from the creek tonguing slowly through the new excavation. Thus the creek had been changed in the first place and now it was changed back. Let Loren do what he would. There would soon be substantial water on the boundary line of the old Rocking A — water for which men in the past had broken their hearts.

TWELVE

He managed to get back to the cabin before dawn. He paused at the well, drew up a pail of water, then stripped to the belt and thoroughly washed himself. He was hungry now, and dog-tired, and he remembered that this was the day when his neighbors would come for a meeting. He was eager for that and the chance to explain to them what he had done about the scattered cattle and hand over the receipts he had got from Donner's bank.

Stopping at the chopping block, he picked up wood then went on into the cabin. Dawn was breaking above the hills, the first pale light coming in over the Horseshoe. He went to the stove and lifted a lid, then a voice spoke from behind him.

"Drop the wood, Ute — and shove up your hands. This time you'd better behave."

"Brig!" Ute gasped. He had no choice but to obey. He let the wood fall to the floor, raised his arms slowly, then defiantly turned around.

Brig had pressed himself behind the door as Ute came in, not stepping forth until Ute's back was turned to the stove. In the pale morning light, Ute could see the gun Brig held. The grin on the man's face was sneering and triumphant. Probably he did not know that word of his escape had reached here ahead of him. He thought he had delivered a more jolting surprise than he had. That seemed to gratify the vanity of

165

the little man, and Brig came forward and took Ute's gun.

"Reported to Loren yet?" Ute drawled.

"How does it come," Brig said, "that you always mention Loren? The Taplan family so big that a man can't cut his own capers in this country?"

"You're too picayune to cut your own," Ute retorted. "What do you want?"

"You."

"How come?"

"You're coming with me on a ride," Brig said. "The how-come is my business."

"We'll have to ride double unless you brought an extra horse. I don't have a one on hand."

"Then we'll ride double. Ute, have you handed out them bank receipts?"

"A smart man would lose no time about that, Brig."

In spite of the man's repeated denials, he thought, Brig had just tied himself to Loren and Donner with that question. He could not know about the receipts unless one of them had told him and sent him here to get them — or, which seemed the case, to get Ute Taplan. Ute had a sudden clammy feeling. He had hidden the receipts carefully and now faced the prospect of having Brig try to sweat them out of him.

"You ain't passed them out or you wouldn't look so scared," Brig taunted. "But don't worry. Not yet. You don't have to dig them up for me. If I snake you out of here, you won't give them out to nobody. That's all it takes and I'm in a rush."

"Who murdered Hines and Rudeen?" Ute retorted. "And sprung you? Was it your own gang or Joe Lake? It had to be one or the other. You aren't man enough to cut a thing like that alone."

"I got away, didn't I? Now, you shut your trap. Go ahead and fix breakfast, though. I come a long piece, and we got a longer one to travel. We better eat. You cook. I'm going to hold this persuader on you, and it wouldn't trouble me much to have to use it."

Ute welcomed the chance to cook or do anything to delay the showdown. Yet he doubted that he would be given any chance to take the jump away from Brig again.

He said, "What do you want to eat? We can eat high on the hog if you've got the time. I just got a load of groceries out from town. I don't suppose you've fared too well in the back country. How about some hot cakes and bacon?"

"Go ahead," Brig said, and he looked interested. "And while you're about it, you can tell me what went off over at the crick just before you come in."

"Dynamite."

Brig straightened, puzzlement creasing his brow. "You mean you tampered with that water?"

"You might say I only untampered it, Brig. I took back what belonged to Rocking A all through the years it didn't have it." Ute had not wanted Loren to learn of his night's achievement so soon, but now he desperately needed a break. Brig looked worried and seemed to feel the matter to be something he should convey to Loren at once. Prodding him, Ute added, "Why don't we go by Pick and get me a horse — on our way to wherever we're going?"

"Might do that," Brig said.

"Which makes twice that you've admitted your ties with Loren."

"So what?" Brig said defiantly. "You knew already, and you still can't prove anything."

He turned moody, after that. Ute went ahead with the cooking, and he took his time. The little gunman had seated himself at the table, well out of Ute's reach and with his thoughtful eyes observing Ute's every move.

When Ute had their breakfast ready, Brig said, "I'll eat first, unless you want to do it

168

standing there at the stove. I ain't giving you another chance to rush me, man. When you damned Injuns get sore, you don't care if you live or die."

Ute put the food on the table. When he stepped back, Brig began to eat with one hand, his cold, intent gaze rarely leaving Ute for more than a second. But he was hungry and scarcely seemed to chew the food before he swallowed it. When he had satisfied himself, he wiped his mouth on his sleeve and pushed back his chair.

"Your turn," he said.

Ute knew by then that he was not going to get a break here, and he had only a dim hope of getting one even if Brig took him off by way of Pick. Brig had orders and meant to carry them out, but he would not hesitate to kill instantly if endangered. Ute knew he had to go along. He was frightened but made himself sit down calmly at the table and eat his own breakfast.

"We'll go by Pick first," Brig conceded, finally. "Come on. I left my cayuse back across the rise. We'll go and get it."

"Let's go see my white brother," Ute said. He pulled on his filthy shirt, then his hat.

Thereafter he was forced to tramp ahead of Brig to the place where the man had concealed his horse beyond a swell of ground. There Brig said, "Swing up, man. I'll perch behind and shove this gun so hard into your back you'll pooch out in front."

"Nobody," Ute returned, "can get any cockier than a runt with the upper hand."

On Brig's horse they struck out across country for Pick. As they came down upon the place, Brig made Ute halt the horse while he took a long look at what showed in the ranchyard. Then they went on. When they had come down into the yard, presently, Brig slid off hurriedly, eager to get himself beyond Ute's reach.

Although it was still early in the morning, Pick's crew had got busy with the work. But Loren appeared in the doorway of the ranch office, scowling in mixed anger and surprise.

"Damn you, Brig," he said. "Why did you bring him here?"

"Mainly," Brig said, "because I couldn't leave him anywhere, and there's something I figured you'd want to know. Besides, he didn't have any horse, and I want to pick one up."

"You reckless fool. What have you got to tell me?"

"Ute done some dynamiting, last night. At the crick."

"He what?"

"I told you," Brig said. "Go look for

yourself. You figured he'd dry up quick over there. But he won't unless you do something pronto. Now am I such a damned fool?"

Loren swung a hard attention on Ute, who was sliding painfully from the saddle. It was almost as if he had been struck a physical blow, and Ute hoped desperately to checkmate the man and knock in the head whatever plan Brig was carrying out for him.

Brig said, "I'm going to get him a horse. You watch him while I'm gone. He'd carve out your guts if he could, and you know it."

Loren seemed to share that fear. It gave Ute a strange sense of aversion to see his supposed brother's hand go down and bring up his pistol. Yet Loren's eyes began to show the wild aggression that could form in them so easily. Defeat was a poison to him, and he had suffered so many that each new one was magnified out of proportion in his mind. Sensing that something might happen, Brig lingered.

"The sly one," Loren breathed. "Sneaking and treacherous and nothing but a goddam redskin." In his eyes was a streaky glitter of hatred that must have been there from the day Tap brought home his foundling. That had gone deeply into Loren and festered there all through the years. It was an unstable danger in him now.

Ute felt recklessness rise within himself at the taunts. In the slow way that was his own danger signal, he said, "Mebbeso, Loren. But just the same I've always beaten you any way we ever tangled. I could whip you in a fight. I could hobnob with the crew, with them liking to have me with them. The basiners showed you what they thought about you in two elections, and about me. Your best riders quit you to go to work for me at no pay at all. Just hating your guts enough so that nothing else mattered."

Harshly Loren said, "There's one place you lost out, where I reckon it hurts. Olivia used to be mighty sweet on you. Lately I don't think she's been quite so fervent."

"If she's swinging your way, Loren, it isn't you that draws her needle but Pick. I was slow to see how much she thinks of this ranch. If she ever teams with you, it'll be because she thinks that much of becoming the mistress of it. That's what come between us. And if you're stepping into my boots, there, it's only because I stepped out of 'em voluntarily."

It was a bold, heedless thing to say to Loren, and Ute watched the wrath swirl anew in his eyes. Loren reholstered his gun. His shoulders came up, and then he charged.

Ute had expected it, wanted it even while knowing that he was in no condition to fight the man. He ducked back and goaded again, "Just your size, Loren. Fighting me with your little gunhand· there to see you don't get hurt."

"Goddam your soul to hell!" Loren blazed as he wheeled around.

For a moment afterward they only stared at each other. Maybe for that brief time Loren reconsidered. But the tempest in his brain and emotions had its way with him. He drove in again.

This time Ute met him head on. He took the first force of Loren's blow on the edge of his jaw and let it glance off or it would have floored him. He countered the stiff, swift punch that followed and crossed his own left hand to Loren's jaw. It drove the man back off-balance and awkward, but Ute could not follow it up. Besides, he wanted to see how long Loren's courage would last.

It lasted. Loren was all but berserk now, and he steadied himself. He came in feinting and jabbing, guarding himself at last. Ute had lost track of Brig but knew that the man was still there, watching in grim satisfaction but ready to take things back into his own hands if this thing came out wrong.

Ute sparred a moment. They had fought

again and again in their boyhood, and he had known Loren's style in and out. Loren's fighting was always a case of outbursting temper, a momentarily heedless onslaught of killing wrath. Ute saw an opening and drove a fist through it, landing it against Loren's belly. Before he had recovered, he had taken Loren's smash on his mouth. He tasted blood but covered himself sufficiently against the man's sudden drive to protect it from another crushing blow.

Then he went in on his own determined rush. He hooked rights and lefts at Loren, who tied him up with his arms while they turned full about. Loren tried to knee him in that close huddle and used enough force to send a wrench of pain through Ute. Then Loren hit him full and hard on the hurt rib. Ute emitted a gusty sound of pain as he reeled back.

Loren came on in full assault. The pain seemed to paralyze Ute's whole right side, rendering his arm all but useless to him. He shoved with the other hand, hauling in gagging breaths and trying only to hold Loren off. But Loren thought he saw his course. He kept moving sideways, trying to get around for another attack on the weak side he had discovered.

Ute tried desperately to make his will flow

down along his arm into the fist. Then, aware that he stood on the verge of ruin, he squared himself on Loren, who came forward just as Ute shot out his previously hampered fist. The action caught Loren completely unawares. Ute felt the man's teeth rip into his knuckles; he heard the snap of Loren's head. Both of Loren's arms went up in a helpless way. He came down hard. He tried just once to rise, then sank back and lay still.

Out of the swirling obscurities about Ute came Brig's cool voice.

"That wasn't a bad show, Ute. But what good did it do you?"

Ute looked then at the gun in Brig's hand. In a torn, panting way, he said, "Plenty."

"Come on," Brig said. "We'll go and get you a horse."

THIRTEEN

Ute staggered as he walked ahead of Brig toward the day corral. There the man ordered him into the enclosure to snake out a mount. Ute had trouble in doing it, and that was not feigned. He nearly keeled over before he got a saddle cinched onto the horse, but Brig was afraid to come close enough to help.

Ute took a long last look at Pick headquarters, the scene of so many years of his life. Then, Brig behind him, he rode out from there for what stood to be the last time. Brig headed north, toward the badlands. Ute kept himself steady by centering his thoughts on the simple matter of survival through whatever lay ahead. He was still waiting for a halfway hopeful break.

Two hours thereafter they had begun to thread their way into the roughs. By then Ute had recalled Curly and his men, at work in here somewhere, trying to gather the scattered horses and cattle. It dawned on him that Brig had not mentioned Curly. It was possible that he did not know that the party was in here. However, Ute failed to see where that could help him now. The malpais was a vast and difficult country. Men could rattle around in it for weeks without encountering each other.

Already he was growing bewildered by the broken, tangled nature of the roundabout. But Brig seemed to know his way thoroughly and pressed forward without hesitation. There was little vegetation, and the rock trapped heat and radiated it until the air was smothering. Ute had worked all night, had had his fight with Loren, and an unwelcome torpor settled on him so that, again and again, he caught himself napping in the saddle. He lost track of time.

Then all at once the country opening before them brought him fully alert. For a long while they had been threading the bottoms of deep and narrow canyons. Suddenly the way ahead broke open. His bloodshot eyes perceived grass and a distant line of trees that bespoke a water course. Slowly he identified it, a place called Devil's Garden, which he had heard about but never seen because of its deep isolation. As they came out of the canyon, he got a second start when he discerned cattle in this mountain hole.

"So you've got a real rustlers' hangout," he said to Brig. All along he had figured that activity to be a blind to cover more important actions. A hope spurted in him, desperate and perhaps forlorn. There were a lot of steers in here, and he could now detect loose horses in the same vicinity. If the road herd had been brought here intact, Curly was bound to find this place and might have discovered it already.

Brig did not respond to Ute's comment, and they struck out across the coulee floor. Soon Ute saw smoke rising in a scarcely discernible wisp above the forward trees. He observed hobbled horses there, presently, and knew that he and Brig were riding in upon an outlaw camp. A half dozen men stood there, watching. Ute's heart sank. They would be too many even for the uncertain help that might come from Curly.

"Ute Taplan!" a man said, as they rode up. "What the hell are you doing with him, Brig? And why bring him here?"

"Keep your shirt on, Ace," Brig said. "We've got to keep him hidden a while."

"Then hide him in the ground."

"Not yet," Brig answered. "Loren said we were only to hold him here till we get other orders."

Ace scowled. He was a tall, swart man, a total stranger to Ute. So were the other five men, and they all had the hard-faced, shifty-eyed look of ridge runners.

Reading something of the cause for the frown on Ace's face, Ute said, "I heard of this place but never thought of it. Maybe the sheriff has heard and will think of it. Or somebody else."

"Maybe that won't matter a damn, Ute," Brig said. "You just behave yourself and you won't find us bad company for a while."

Ute intended to remain docile for as long as he could do so. His main hope was Curly and the men with him. He said, "Can a fellow get some sleep?" and nobody objected.

He got a couple of saddle blankets and spread them out under a tree. Brig told him to eat first from the kettle of stew on the fire. Ute did, not hungry but realizing that he had to build up his strength. Afterward he slept, finding it dark when he awakened.

He knew that a camp like this would be under the guard of more than one quick-triggered man. He lay quietly, remembering that this was the night when the little ranchers were to have come to Rocking A. He wondered what they would surmise from his unexplained absence and what they would do. But mostly he worried over why Loren wanted him kept hidden. He had not arrived at any definite conclusion when, out of his deep exhaustion, he fell asleep again.

When he opened his eyes the next time, it was the dawn of a new day. Here on the wasteland oasis, the rocky hills stood far enough apart to make the heat less oppressive. The morning air was almost cool. The outlaw camp was already stirring. He saw men eating their breakfast. Except for mounting guard on the approaches to the place, they had little to do to occupy their time.

Rising, Ute saw that a fair-sized creek ran past the camp. Eroded country was given to unexpected springs and streams that ran a distance only to vanish into the earth from which they came. He walked down to the creek, quenched his thirst and washed himself. He returned to the camp, and Brig's nod at the kettle told him to eat again. Ute did, afterward rolling himself a cigarette and smoking it while he finished his coffee.

It had now been nearly twenty-four hours since he and Brig had entered the malpais. Ute was caught between stubborn hope and sudden gusts of despair. Curly was his one hope of escaping here, but there was a very real risk of Curly's running into a gun trap set by the outlaws. Ute kept teasing that in his mind but failed to see what he could do to prevent such a disaster. Yet Curly was smart and had ridden for Pick for a long while. If sign or his own suspicions led him close to this place, he was capable of adding things up for himself.

It gave Ute an eerie feeling to hear the report of fired guns come in the midst of his worrying. Every man in the camp was on his feet at the first shot, all of them staring eastward toward one of the portals into the place. Over there was a sheer rock rim, broken in the center. A rifle had been fired, the shots spaced out.

"That's the signal!" Ace shouted. "How come they could get here this soon?"

Brig looked stricken, caught flat-footed. "It ain't the sheriff," he said. "Must be friends of the Injun's."

"Then kill and get him out of sight," Ace snapped.

"We can't touch him till Loren's got it set. You know that. Come on. Let's see what's up."

Men ran for the hobbled horses down the creek from the camp. But Ute was not optimistic enough to hope that he would be left here alone. Excitement sang in him, nonetheless. There had been that burst of shooting, then a complete silence. Maybe the outlaw guard was just jumpy and wanted help in investigating something that had worried him. Or maybe it was Curly skulking around.

Brig, throwing on a saddle, swung and spoke to a man who looked crestfallen as a result but turned back toward the camp. Two minutes later, the others were running their horses in a scattered rush up the length of the creek toward the rim break. Ute figured close and hard. The man ordered back to guard him seated himself morosely on a rock at a safe distance and was watching him with truculence. He did not like this job when there was something bigger afoot.

"Wouldn't they let you play with them?" Ute taunted.

"Shut up."

But the man was not going to be goaded into coming closer. The pound of hoofs faded in the east, then the horsemen disappeared into the rim break. There still had been no more gunfire up there.

Suddenly the guard shoved to a hasty stand. But he was staring to the south in hard intentness. Looking in that direction, Ute saw two horses spill out of the portal by which he and Brig had entered the coulee. They pulled up for an instant, as if getting their bearings, then came on at a rush.

The guard gasped a curse, then said, "They're friends of yours, all right. Come on — we're fading out of here."

"Not me," Ute retorted. "But if you know what's good for you, you'll fan your own tail. There must be others right behind them."

The man seemed to share that opinion. He could not stop the riders coming at the camp, even if he tried to fight them off. He knew he would have to shoot his prisoner if he insisted on taking him along, which could only delay him and would be contrary to the orders Brig had given. He hesitated only a second, then bolted to where a horse stood watching the onrushing pair. He did not try to saddle but swung up and went streaking toward the eastern rim break.

Ute knew by then that the newcomers were Curly Jackson and Slim Trawn. They nearly turned in pursuit of the running guard, but Ute yelled and waved his arms, drawing them on toward the camp. There was no time to lose, and he did not have to be told what had taken place. Curly's other men — Dory and Bill — had raised a scare at the east gate while Curly and Slim came in from the south. It had worked, and Ute was saddling himself a horse by the time the two came up.

Curly yelled, "By damn, Ute, you're the last man I ever expected to find in here! What happened?"

"Come on," Ute returned. "That galoot will have the whole bunch after us in a minute." He swung to the saddle. "How about Bill and Dory? They going to need our help?"

"Maybe," Curly said. "But they were only supposed to show themselves at the other side, then hightail it and try to draw the lobos out of the coulee. All we wanted was a look at the steers in here, and maybe a chance to pick up a few horses."

By then they were riding for the southern exit. They continued for a half hour after leaving the place before Curly pulled down his sweating horse. He was tight-faced, and his cocky manner was pure front when he said, "That's all the fun I want for one day, believe me."

"How'd you get past the south guard?" Ute asked.

"Sneaked up on him. Finding you was sheer luck."

"But we've had some mighty bad luck, too," Ute said. "Brig got away and is back with this bunch. His men sprang him from Stub and Vic. They killed both of them."

"Oh, no," Curly said and was silent for a long moment. Then, in a grim voice, he added, "Let's get it settled here and now."

Ute shook his head. "They outnumber us too bad. On top of that Loren and Lake are trying to pull some kind of a stunt out in the basin. Lake must have quit the drive and come back. I heard Brig mention his being in Starbow. We've got to work fast, and we'll need all the help we can scare up. First, though, we'd better get hold of Bill and Dory."

"We were to meet back at our camp,"

Curly said. "Let's go — and hope we find them there."

They were successful in that, although not until the end of another hour's riding in which Curly and Slim backtracked themselves. But the other two punchers were in the camp they had set up at a water hole. They were as surprised as Curly had been to see Ute.

"Well, there's no time to set around," Slim said. "We know where the stuff all is. The next thing's to latch onto it. Let's get out of here."

The camp was struck immediately. Thereafter the party, leading a pack pony now, began the tortuous business of finding its way out of the badlands without being discovered by Brig's searching men. The shadows were stretching out when finally the little party broke out into Horseshoe Basin.

Ute said, "You boys go on to Rocking A. I'll take a turn past Ross Ide's. Ginny called a meeting at my place, last night. I'd like to find out what they done when I didn't put in an appearance."

Curly and his companions rode on. Ute turned his horse east, striking a direct course across the sage-studded openland. An hour after that he rode up to Ide's

185

headquarters.

Ginny had seen him coming and was waiting in the yard, showing surprise at seeing him but also wearing a deeper look of concern. "Where have you been, Ute?" she called.

"Did you have your meeting?"

"It was brought together," she said in a fierce voice. "But your brother and Joe Lake showed up with the sheriff. Ute, they turned it into a virtual grand jury investigation. I'm scared to death."

Ute swung in deep weariness from the saddle. In a gentle voice, he said, "Take it easy, Ginny. Just tell me what happened."

She said, "We were all waiting there on Rocking A, figuring you'd be home any time. Then those three showed up. It seems that Sheriff Breckenridge had contacted Lake in Starbow, where Lake was waiting for him, and got his ear filled full of lies. You're in terrible danger, Ute — the sheriff's after you right now."

"Calm down, now," Ute said, although he did not know who he was to be offering such advice, for apprehension was pouring all through him.

"Well, they'd come to Rocking A after you. Your friends were pretty riled about it, and the sheriff sort of hashed it all over again, explaining. Loren claims Brig's a private range detective he hired to check on rustling he knew was going on all summer. That Brig's investigations proved you were doing it. That you had a gang in the malpais."

"That might make sense," Ute said, "if he can explain why I'd rustle on myself. Tap was even alive, last summer."

"Loren claimed you rustled on Pick for a blind. That your big play was the one that just happened — latching onto the road herd. He says that's why he pulled Pick out. That he didn't warn the others because he figured to stop it before they'd been hurt and wanted to use that herd for bait."

Ute nodded. "They've got to cover themselves, and that sounds pretty good when you first hear it. But it won't hold up."

"Why won't it?" Ginny said bitterly. "Every man that stuck with Pick will swear to whatever Loren says."

"I can prove I bought that road herd voluntarily. After it had been jumped and lost. Why would I do that and pay market prices when a rustler couldn't get that much?"

"*Can* you prove it, though?"

"If they haven't found the receipts I got from the bank." He told her, then, what had happened to him, concluding, "They figured taking care of me would take care of those receipts, me being the only one who knew where I hid them. Do you know if Loren got out a warrant for me?"

"Yes," Ginny said. "When they didn't find you home, Loren and Lake claimed you'd hit for the tall timber. So the sheriff formed a posse."

"From the basiners?"

She smiled grimly. "Not by a long shot. They told the sheriff he could lock them up, but they weren't riding on any posse out after you. So Loren volunteered Pick's crew. It was just what he wanted. They'll kill you on sight if they get a chance — and all in the name of the law."

Nothing could come from Loren any more that was surprising to Ute. He said, "They latched onto me to have me handy for it."

"Oh, Ute."

It was not his initiative when she came to him, placed her cheek quietly against his chest, and let go of the tears she did not want him to see. But it was his responsibility when he tipped back her head and placed his lips to her mouth. The kiss was swift and sweet and different from those that had come from his old male interest. Here was strength and courage and loyalty beyond a man's deserts — all in this one girl. He had never needed to probe the question of where he stood with her, to weigh and wonder at her motives or speculate upon her capacity for love.

Then, when her quiet crying was relieved, he said, "We're not licked yet. The basin steers are in the malpais on grass and water and in one bunch. It's going to be quicker getting them back if not any easier."

"First you've got to prove that Brig did the rustling and not you."

He nodded. "You'd better come with me to Rocking A. If those receipts are still where I put them, you're the only one who could take them to the sheriff in any kind of safety."

"I'm ready."

Ute caught her a horse while she hurried into the house. Ross Ide seemed to be having one of his bad days, for he still did not appear. By the time Ute had the horse saddled, Ginny was outside again and ready to ride. She rose lightly to the leather, and they headed for Rocking A.

FOURTEEN

They rode swiftly, neither talking, each deeply preoccupied by the grave situation confronting them. When they thundered into the ranchyard of the old Arbuckle spread, Ute in his eagerness swung from his horse and was half running when he entered the cabin.

Curly and the boys were there, lingering over a meal they had prepared for themselves. They straightened with hard stares at his haste, to which he paid no immediate attention. Looking about, he could see no signs of the place having been ransacked in his absence and he felt a little easier.

He went directly to the shelf above the store, now stocked with the groceries that had been brought out from town. There was a case of tomatoes stacked there. He had to lift a couple of cans before he found one light enough to suit him. He turned it bottom side up. There was a long slit in the bottom, pried open and through which he had drained the can. After rising the container, he had slipped the bank receipts inside.

One glance told him that the can was now empty. He groaned as he turned around. He said, "They went over the place with a fine-tooth comb. Probably after my ruckus with Loren. Must have got him worried that I'd beat Brig, somehow, too."

"They're gone?" Ginny said in sinking despair.

"Gone."

"Oh, Ute — what will we do?"

Ginny dropped onto a chair at the table. The punchers, while not fully understanding as yet, looked grim and concerned. In a halting voice, Ute told them how he had been made a fugitive overnight. Since they had sided him, they also were in jeopardy of the law.

"Now — wait a minute," he said, right in the middle of it. "Maybe we can still prove that I bought that road herd. I told you I planned to do it before I left your house, Ginny. I made the checks out there on blanks I borrowed from your dad."

Ginny shook her head. "That wouldn't prove you put them in the bank, though."

"There's a witness to that, too," Ute said, a little excited by then. "Not Donner's clerks — they'd be too scared to tell the truth. I mean Olivia. She was over here, afterward, and ripped into me for buying those cattle. She had to learn that through Loren and him from Donner. And she'll tell the sheriff exactly who and what."

"You think she would?" Ginny said.

"Why not?"

Ginny looked at him through narrowed

eyelids for a long moment, then said, "I wouldn't say this if things weren't so desperate. But if I were you, I wouldn't bet my safety on it."

Angrily, he said, "What reason have you got to say that?"

"I think Olivia made up her mind which of the Taplan boys is going to come out on top."

It was the first time he had ever felt like hitting a woman, and he wanted to hit Ginny. Yet when he looked at Curly and the other punchers he had the shocking realization that they were inclined to agree with her.

Stiffly, he said, "If you're interested in helping, Ginny, here's what I thought. Me and the boys will have to lay low. You could get one of the basiners to help. Then somebody see Sheriff Breckenridge and somebody Olivia. Have them both at Donner's bank when it opens tomorrow morning. I'll be there."

"Not unless we side you," Curly said promptly.

"Damn it," Ute blazed, "go ahead and think Olivia's a turncoat. I don't believe it, and she's the only chance I've got to clear myself of Loren's charges. And there's more ·· than that involved. If they get away with this, and Donner can kill those deposits, they're riding high in the saddle again. They'll scatter that herd when it's served its purpose and go right on and take over the basin."

"I'll do my best," Ginny said. "But I'm warning you. I don't think it'll work."

"You just worry about getting the sheriff and Olivia to the bank in the morning."

"All right," Ginny said, and he knew that his roughness had hurt her deeply. "They'll be there if I have to rope and drag them. Only — Curly, you boys go to town with him, no matter what he says."

"You can count on that, Ginny," Curly told her, and his eyes were no longer friendly as he glanced at Ute.

Ginny left hurriedly and did not look at Ute again.

Gruffly, Curly said, "You were pretty rough-shot there, man. She was right about one thing, anyhow. Going to town's sticking your neck in a hang noose. Don't you forget there's more than cattle thieving involved in what they've charged you with. It includes murder. If you don't sell your medicine to the sheriff, don't think he's going to let you leave town."

"If I can't prove my ease, there's no use in my trying to leave."

"All right. But we're going with you."

"Then come along."

They had an early breakfast, the next morning, leaving for town immediately afterward. Although they had kept a constant watch, they had not been disturbed during the night. Maybe the posse — all Pick men, he had been told — had gone into the badlands coulee, learned what had transpired and decided that the so-called fugitives were still somewhere in the breaks. If the sheriff was with the posse, he would be hard for a basiner to locate. And if the officer was towed off, Loren would be suspicious and might go to Starbow with the sheriff.

But Ute knew that Loren would prefer to run the posse he had himself provided, and would try to dissuade the sheriff from remaining with it. There was no question that, now he had turned his supposed brother into a ridge runner, Loren would want him killed on sight. So Ute felt there was a good chance that Breckenridge was letting Pick do the riding and canyon beating.

He was no fool, Ute knew. He must have heard enough from the little basiners, at that meeting, to make him want to hear more of their side without Loren around to explain everything so readily. If he was right about that, Ute felt that Ginny, or whoever she got to help her, had had time to locate the officer.

Riding through that cool morning, it struck him how completely he was depending on both Ginny and Olivia. He knew as well as he knew anything that Ginny would not fail him unless she died trying. But he could trust Olivia to the same extent. He knew that, too. They had disagreed on a few things, lately. But Olivia would not let him down, with his life depending upon it.

She knew by now that Loren had tied, trying to frame a man who could be his own brother. She probably had never heard that the basin widely suspected Loren of having engineered her own father's death. She would not have to know, even, that Loren was guilty of the crimes with which he had charged Ute. The fact that Loren was lying in that one matter would tip the balance, and she would tell the sheriff the truth. That, Ute thought, would be the first step on the road to his and Olivia's getting back together again.

Speaking his conclusion aloud, Ute said, "Unless Breckenridge is in Starbow ahead of us, we better not go in. There's a way we could tell. We'll stop by Crosscut. Ginny would be sure she'd tagged the sheriff before she'd go see Olivia, feeling about her the way she does."

"Good idea to check," Curly agreed.

They did not wait until they had come to the Crosscut turn-off but struck across country from that point. Olivia was not home. But old Cash Parmody, one of her punchers, was working in the ranch blacksmith shop. He said, "She went to town. Ginny Ide was by here with Sheriff Breckenridge. Olivia didn't like it a little bit, either."

Ute could not help sliding a glance to Curly, whose features wore a sudden frown.

"The sheriff's in Starbow, anyhow," Curly said. "If you still want to go in."

"Why not?"

Curly shrugged.

They rode on at the same unhurried gait because they had to make sure that the others arrived in town ahead of them. Starbow, when they reached it, was just opening up for business. The hitchracks were empty except for three saddle horses at the bar in front of the bank.

Ginny and her companions had not yet entered Donner's place of business but stood on the sidewalk. They were all watching the oncoming riders. Swinging down,

196

Ute smiled first at Olivia, then at the sheriff. He found himself too riled as yet to include Ginny. Yet he took a close enough look to see that her cheeks were pale, her shoulders rigid. Then his own tension mounted when neither of the other two returned his greeting.

Breckenridge was stern-faced, and the eyes that watched Ute were wintry. Olivia looked off in the other direction, withdrawn, disturbed and a little defiant even. She did not like what she was being forced to do, but Ute could not help that. She had to do it.

"Ginny explained the thing to you?" he asked them. The sheriff nodded guardedly, but Olivia did not respond at all.

"Don't worry about us," Curly said.

Looking at Curly, Ute said, "You and the boys stay out here."

Ute had trouble with his breathing when he went into the bank. He had a sense of walking on quicksand, which was not logical. He had two witnesses who could give the lie to Loren's charges — charges that Donner was sure to back up. He had nothing to worry about at all.

He walked straight toward Donner's office, the others following. But the banker had been warned and must have been told of the sheriff's waiting outside with Ginny and Olivia. Now he showed only a perfunctory interest.

He said, "Well, what can I do for you, Sheriff?"

Moving politely, he ushered the women to seats. He gave Breckenridge the chair beside his desk, and he left Ute standing with an easy insolence that bespoke supreme confidence.

Breckenridge stared at Donner through a thoughtful moment. Tall, gaunt and gray, he was range-hardened and well aware of the unpredictability of men. Ute did not know what he saw in the banker's bland face, for the sheriff's own betrayed nothing whatever.

"I don't have the papers to force a search of your books, Donner," the sheriff said. "But I hope you'll cooperate. I'm going to ask a question or two. It's been claimed that Ute Taplan bought that missing road herd the day after it was jumped. And that he deposited payment here in the name of the owners. If he done so before he knew he'd been charged with rustling, it's a big point in his favor."

Donner let his eyes widen. "It would be, if he done so. Who claims that he did — Ute?"

"The point is — did he?"

"Why," Donner said agreeably, "he could

have, although I'd think my clerks would tell me about it. Buying a herd that's been lost to rustlers is a mite out of the ordinary. You don't need any court order, Sheriff, to see my books. We'll check on that." He got up again and walked out.

Olivia was without expression, without motion in her body except for a shallow run of breath. Although Ute kept trying to catch her eye, she was careful to avoid that. But the sheriff must have questioned her at Crosscut. She must have said enough to persuade him to go through with what Ginny had asked. Ute wasn't worried, for he understood the dreadful position he had forced her into.

Donner was soon back. The clerk who followed him was the one who had accepted the deposits — Henry Morse — and he looked uneasy. He carried a bound ledger which he placed on Donner's desk. Wetting a thumb, the banker leafed through the pages, found a sheet he wanted and shook his head.

Looking up at Breckenridge, he said, "This is Ute's account. I bought an option on Pick from him a while back. It shows that deposit. Been charged with a couple of checks. Henry says one was to the feed store, the other to the mercantile. That's it

— unless there's something that hasn't been posted yet. Is there, Henry?"

Henry Morse shook his head. He was not half as confident as Donner but would say anything the man wanted. He fidgeted with his black cuffs.

"Well," said Donner, "there's still a chance we made a mistake. Something might show up in the accounts he says should have received the credit. Name a few, Ute, and we'll see."

"No use wasting time," Ute retorted. "You got hold of the receipts, Donner. The transactions were never put through. But here's something you might not know. Loren told Olivia about me buying that herd. She lit into me for it. Loren had to learn it from you. There was no other way he could have. That proves I did what I claim."

Breckenridge looked at Olivia, who pulled back her head. Quietly, he said, "Do you stand on what you said at the ranch, ma'am?"

"Of course." Olivia looked at Ute then, full and hard. "I have no least idea of what he's getting at."

"Let's take it a piece at a time. Did Loren tell you about Ute buying that herd?"

"No."

"Did you ever say anything to Ute in that wise at all?"

"Absolutely not. Loren asked me to ride over and tell him about Hines and Rudeen being killed. I did that, but that's the only time I ever even mentioned that herd to Ute."

"Say anything he might of misconstrued?"

Olivia shook her head. "As a matter of fact, I think he's trying to take advantage of an old friendship. But I won't lie for anybody. I just can't."

In a drawn voice, Ginny said, "I doubted that it would do any good, Ute. But I thought that if she had to face you, she might change that story. So I talked the sheriff into making her come."

"Are you satisfied now?" Olivia said tartly.

"No," Ginny said. "Nor am I the least surprised."

Breckenridge had turned to look at Ute. Quietly, he said, "I've got no choice but to place you under arrest."

"Not by a long shot, Sheriff." Curly stood in the doorway and he had his gun in his hand. His eyes were dangerous, and he kept shaking his head. "Ute, get going."

"Realize what you're doing?" Breckenridge said.

"Better than you do, right now."

Ute knew there was no other way left to him. Looking at Olivia for the briefest instant, he said, "I never knew you a bit better than I knew Tap," and then he went out of the room.

When he reached the bank steps he halted, pulling his own gun while Curly and his men made their own way out. They all crossed the sidewalk on the run and swung to saddle. They left town in a headlong gallop.

Curly called, "Too bad, Ute, but better than getting her."

"Only thing that bothers me," Ute answered, "is the way I tied into Ginny last night."

"You bet. They could peel the hide off that girl, but she'd stick with you. Where now?"

"We're really on the dodge. I reckon it's us for the owl-hoot."

They stopped at Rocking A long enough to make up a pack of provisions and to replenish their supply of shells. They headed on at once for the back country, desperate men without plan or much hope, but hard men and determined.

FIFTEEN

The sun was at its peak. The shadows of the broken country shortened so that the whole land seemed to blaze in fury. At the point where they had separated the previous day, Ute said, "I think we'd better go by Ross Ide's. Him and Ginny are our only chance of keeping in touch with what's going on. We got help on our side, don't forget. All the men who defied the law and refused to ride in a posse."

Ross' bad back had again confined him to his rocking chair. He listened grimly to Ute's account of what had happened in Starbow. In a voice heavy with worry, he said, "I reckon you did the only thing you could. But breaking arrest makes you doubly wanted. With the sheriff's posse made up of Pick men and maybe even them owlhooters of Brig's. You boys better take yourselves far off and let the rest of us try to get it straightened out."

Ute shook his head. "Killing me would only take care of one man, and Loren's got more than that to cut, Ross. The basin knows where its steers are, now. So does the sheriff. The stuff could still be driven to the railroad in time to upset the scheme for taking over the rest of the basin. I'm scared to death that Loren will have Brig scatter that herd, after what's happened, to knock that possibility in the head."

"You couldn't stop it," Ide said. "And you'd only get yourself killed trying to."

"If you'll loan me a blank, Ross," Ute said, "I want to write another check. I got more money in Donner's bank than I figured and I want to put it to work again."

"Ute, no," Ide said. "You've done enough for us, already."

"It's not charity, Ross. Only life insurance I'd leave if something happened to me. Otherwise Loren would get that money, and maybe he's already got his eye on it. You have Ginny and the sheriff go and deposit this check in your own account, Breckenridge as a witness. If anything happens to me, you make the necessary mortgage payments to save the little outfits. Don't argue, man. After all, it's only collecting damages from Pick and using it to save yourselves from Loren Taplan."

"That means a lot to you, don't it, Ute?" Ide said softly. "All right, son, we'll do it your way."

Ute wrote a check for a little less than what he figured he still had in the bank, leaving Donner no excuse to refuse payment. He told Ide approximately where he and his companions could be found in case of a new emergency.

Finally, not caring that his saddlemates were listening, he said, "And the biggest thing of all, Ross. I wish I could tell her, but it might be a while before I get a chance. You tell Ginny I wasn't hurt a bit there in the bank. Only set free for good."

"I'll do that," Ross said, his eyes soft and lively. "Because I know how glad she'll be to hear that."

Then Ute rode on with his companions. "You know, Ute," Curly reflected, "I've never seen a man cut out like you. Nobody could get ten dollars out of Loren unless he stood to get eleven back. It's a queer thing."

"He's a Taplan," Ute said cheerfully.

"You don't feel bad about that, any more?"

"Hell no. My folks are in Oregon or California, probably, or maybe they died in an Indian attack at the time I was found by the Paiutes. I'll never know who I am, likely. But I know what I am, and that's all that counts."

"Yeah, man," said Curly. "Don't know who I am, either. From what the folks who raised me could tell me, I might have been dance hall get. I showed up on their door-step one morning, newborn and yelling my head off. We got one thing on mules, anyhow, son. They got ancestors, but we can have posterity."

No man grew so familiar with these badlands that he felt at home in their deeper parts. But Ute and his party had their own tracks to follow as long as daylight lasted. He had to put the past behind him, now, and think ahead to what must next be attempted. With darkness, the moon rose and starlight sifted down upon the breaks. It seemed to him to be an eternal ride, even to the place where Curly and his boys had made their previous camp. When they reached that place, they halted, although not yet decided to lay over for the night.

Ute said, "I got no right to throw your lives into the pot, boys. But it seems to me we've got to keep them from scattering that herd. They'll do it and claim we did to get rid of evidence against us."

"Small chance of taking it over," Curly reflected.

"But a couple of good marksmen at either entrance to the coulee could keep it bottled up a while. I didn't feel like asking the basiners to come in. But I reckon they'll do it on their own, and before very long."

"Seems so to me," Curly said. "And who'd rather live than put another knot in Loren's tail?" Slim, Bill and Dory nodded their heads in agreement.

"Then you come with me, Slim," Ute said. "We'll take the south side of the hole. The other boys can have the east. But we've got another meal earned, and I reckon we'd better collect it before we separate."

Although impatient to get on with their self-assigned task, the others agreed as to the wisdom of that. They ate cold from the saddlebags, afterward lingering long enough to smoke their cigarettes.

Curly said, "Loren won't try to scatter the steers till he hears you broke arrest in Starbow. Donner will get that word to him fast, I reckon, and that will bring Pick in here on the jump. They'd come into the coulee from your side, Ute, and you're trying to hog the fun."

"But they'd scatter the herd to the east," Ute pointed out. "The way it come into the coulee. If they run it south, there'd be too much chance of it spilling back into the Horseshoe. We'll try to keep Pick out of the coulee, entirely. But if it gets in, or we do any shooting and pull the outlaws down on us, too, then you've got a chance to hit them from behind."

Curly accepted the plan, then, and they separated. Riding out with Slim, Ute was not discounting the size of the undertaking, and more than once he had to put down a rising dread. The distance from their stopping place to the south portal of the coulee was not great. There would be a guard to overcome there before he and Slim could take post where he wanted to wait. They let their horses slow to be quieter as they drew into that vicinity. Finally Ute pulled down, Slim swinging his mount in beside him.

Neither man needed to speak. Swinging down from the saddle, they tied the horses to the low-growing brush, then took saddle carbines from the boots to reinforce their hand guns. Each man took along his catch rope. Slim had been over the ground with Curly when they had overcome the previous guard. Ute let him lead the way.

Slim angled up the talus until they came in under the sheer lip of the rocky canyon wall. Shadows and detritus that was thickly studded with boulders gave them ample cover, and they moved with slow care. Once Slim paused to listen through a long, intent moment.

Turning back toward Ute, he whispered, "Whoever's on watch this time will be jumpy now. Doubt that he'll be where we could rope him. We'd better bait the son. You cut across that traverse, then come in on the other side. Make just enough racket to get him interested but not really scared."

"Good as done," Ute said.

He started at once, angling back down to the canyon floor. He was not too taken with the idea of losing contact with Slim just then, but it had to be done this way. He crossed to the far side of the narrow canyon and went along that talus. It took only a few minutes, afterward, to gain a lateral canyon that came in from toward the Horseshoe. He turned right at that juncture, skulking through the rock. Presently he could see the jaws of the portal that gave into the coulee, itself.

The guard would be far enough this way to sound a warning to the outlaw camp and make a stand before the portal could be breached. Ute drew no challenge, however, and he could not make out a human figure in the obscure shapes ahead. He paused presently, picked up a pebble and tossed it against the cliff wall.

It made a distinct click when it hit, then a small clatter as it tumbled down. A man's voice bawled instantly, "Who's that?"

Ute kept quiet, motionless. The guard did not call out again, but presently Ute saw a figure moving slowly toward him in the forward distance. He hoped that Slim had managed to get himself set. Then the guard stopped moving and paused through minutes before he turned around and started back the other way. Ute still saw nothing of Slim.

The only way he knew that the long-coupled puncher had chipped in was when the guard was jerked sidewise and down. A rope had done that, Ute knew, and he bolted forward. Slim was handling his way down his tightened catch rope as if he had just thrown a steer. The guard was yelling and cursing, but no sound short of a gunshot would carry as far as the camp. His pinned arms kept him from shooting.

"Shut up," Slim said, "before I shove a rock down your noisy throat."

The guard fell quiet then, aware that two men had come upon him instead of one and not knowing but what there were more. Ute took the slack in Slim's rope and went to work on the guard. He did a careful job of trussing the man, then he shoved his bandanna handkerchief into the man's mouth. Afterward they carried him up among the concealing rocks and left him there.

"Hope the other boys made out as well," Ute said. "Now, you take this side of the canyon, Slim, and I'll take the other. We'll get a little warning if anybody tries to come in — Loren or whoever it is won't see any need to keep quiet. We'll try to take them if we can. If not — then we've got a fight and the lobos will be in on our backs. Want to call for your time?"

"Yeah," Slim said. "The same as you do. I'm glad that side canyon comes in here. If we can't cut the mustard, that's how we might get away."

They moved on into their final positions, where they could command the length of the canyon toward the coulee and also back in the direction of Horseshoe Basin. They might not have long to wait, or it might be hours, but Ute felt strongly that this would be the first place to receive attention after what had happened in Starbow. He settled himself, alert but resting as best he could. He could no longer see Slim, and again the night's loneliness came in upon the canyon.

It seemed to him that he had been there all of two hours when a sound sharply hooked his attention. Rising to a half stand, he peered down the canyon reach toward the basin. The source of the sound was not yet in evidence. His eyes strained against the night. Again his ears registered something, and now it was the impression of several horses coming on. He scowled. He had hoped that Loren would send only a man or two with a message to Brig to get rid of the herd at once.

He felt certain that it was Pick coming on, although he had to make sure it was not the sheriff or even a party of basiners coming in as he expected. His lips ruled grimly. Across the way from him he could see that Slim had come to a crouch, holding tight to his carbine.

Then three riders came around the slight bend in the canyon, exposing themselves fully to view. Two rode abreast, the other trailing a little behind. Ute felt the muscles of his shoulders pull into tight bands. Both he and Slim lowered themselves out of sight. The sound of the hoof falls, never loud, came closer.

Ute had to use sharp judgment to time his move when he shoved to a stand, calling, "Pull down, men, and shove up your arms! Don't make any noise!"

The trailing rider was still too far behind. But the other two, almost under Ute's position, came to a full stop.

"Ute Taplan!" one of them let out.

Then the thing went to pieces completely. As if energized by that name, the hindmost rider whipped his horse full about. It looked like a bold act of courage until Ute realized it was only fast thinking on the man's part. The warning to keep quiet had been a mistake. It had told that one man that while this entrance was in the hands of the enemy, the coulee was not. The fellow was gambling his life on a hunch that his escape would be considered less dangerous than shots fired to stop him. Ute heard Slim's discerning curse, then the fleeing rider cut out of sight beyond the bulge in the canyon wall.

Ute feared that the others would catch on and follow suit, but they seemed to have no such daring. They had lifted their hands, and he already had seen that both were loyal Pick men. Hastening down the talus, he seized the reins of their mounts.

Breathing more easily then, he said, "Slide down, boys. Be a while before he can get back here with help. And you've got some information we need."

They obeyed with alacrity, Fred Springs and Varsal Tantro, men who had stuck with their spread but obviously were not eager to die or even take a beating on Loren's behalf. Slim Trawn took their guns. They moved the prisoners up into the boulders to where the outlaw guard had been left.

"If you behave and answer some questions," Ute said, "you won't be hurt. Where's Loren and Lake?"

"On Pick," Tantro said.

"What did they send you here for?"

213

"To tell Brig to run off the steers and to help him do it."

"Where's the sheriff?"

Tantro shrugged. "Dunno, and that's a fact."

Slim tied them up while Ute kept them under the cover of his gun. They gagged both men, as well.

Then Slim said tiredly, "Well, the next time we'll have a real force to meet. The way they'll pound it, that'll come in three–four hours. Before then somebody's bound to come out from the lobo camp to change off with the guard we put on ice. We better figure out something real neat or we're in trouble."

"Got to play the cards the way they fall, Slim."

"And I sure wish I was dealing."

It now seemed more important to guard against somebody coming from the camp in the coulee since the outlaws were probably taking two or three hour turns on watch. Ute felt capable of surprising and capturing the man. But suspicion would be aroused in the camp when nobody returned after the change, and he saw no way to meet that situation except head on.

He said, "Slim, it would be better to fight that wild bunch separately than to have it on our backs after Pick gets here in one big bunch."

"Been thinking that myself," Slim said. "Not much sense in guarding this canyon any longer. We know what's bound to come and how much time we've got left. Ought to take over the coulee if we can. But how?"

"The man that got away missed a bet," Ute said. "If he'd fired a few shots after he got around the bend, it would have brought that lobo pack hell a-hiking. Shooting would bring Curly and his boys in behind them. We better catch those curly wolves in a vise before we're caught that way."

"Shoot 'em off," Slim said.

Lifting his carbine, Ute fired three quick shots.

Thereafter he and Slim moved ahead hurriedly to where the canyon broke out into the coulee. There was no question that the shooting had been heard at the outlaw camp. Their horses would be coursing across the sage flat at any moment. He and Slim were scarcely in position when obscure figures appeared against the blobs that identified the stolen cattle. There were half a dozen horses coming, and they moved together. But the oncomers were wary and while still out of rifle range they pulled down and dismounted.

Ute meant to hold them off, pinning them there until Curly could surprise them from the rear. He fired a warning shot to inform them that the whole portal was in the hands of the enemy. He watched them dive for cover in the thinly standing sage. He did not know how many of them had been in the camp this night. But that probably was all of them since they had turned out in toto the other time to answer the emergency shots.

The rustlers did not return his shot immediately. The instincts of fight and flight were always at war in an outlaw. They could not know who had come upon them or in what strength. But if they decided against a fight and to escape through the east portal, they would run into Curly. Ute knew they were thinking it over, then a few exploring shots cracked out.

These Ute and Slim failed to answer in order to encourage the rustlers and make them come in closer. There was another long silence, a nerve-taut wait. Again came a thumping volley from the sagebrush. With the brush and the night, it was hard for anybody to see anything distinctly enough to be sure of a target. The rustlers fired in volleys so that the gunflash would not be in evidence for too long.

Ute was contented to let them be as cautious as they wanted. But it was a wearing ordeal waiting for the help he and Slim had to have from Curly. Once that had materialized, he reasoned, the outlaws would have to bolt for their horses, and he wanted to be in a position to raise hob with them then. He made a signal to Slim, whom he could still see, then began to work his way forward on his belly.

At last the ground brought to him the telltale beat of driving hoofs. Help was coming from the other gate. The rustlers heard it but were too uncertain to take flight at once. Yet the shooting tapered off. Curly was coming in exactly as Ute had surmised, boldly and down the creek. To the rustlers it must have seemed a carefully sprung trap. All at once they were up and racing for their horses.

Ute leaped to his feet. He put his carbine to work, hearing Slim's at his left. He saw a running figure pitch forward and fail to get up again. Ute fired twice more. A man got clear into the saddle of his horse, then fell off on the far side. The animal bolted off. Four other men made it up. They were forced by Curly's fire to charge straight forward, and they came on with blazing guns. Ute went down, unhit but seeking cover. He flung a shot at a horse that whipped past his position, but the horses were soon swallowed by the canyon portal.

"They'll be back," Slim called. "They'll join up with Pick. But it looks like we got possession of the coulee for a while."

Curly and his men came in then. Ute explained the developments to them, concluding, "I'm damned glad you were listening for shooting down our way."

Sixteen

Slim volunteered to remain in the canyon to warn against the return of Pick. Since there was a chance that Loren would use deceptive tactics when he came, Dory Meadows returned to the east portal. The others took the prisoners to the outlaw camp. They built a fire under the pot of cold coffee that hung on a rod there.

Curly said, "We done the only thing we could. But if the sheriff catches us in charge of this camp with a stolen herd all around us, we've set it up real pretty for Loren."

"If Breckenridge shows before Pick," Ute agreed, "we'll simply have to light out. What I'd like to see show up first is a bunch of the little basiners."

"There's a chance."

218

Ute nodded. "Which we don't have time to turn into a certainty by sending somebody out for help."

"Well," said Curly, "you told Ross Ide what we're up to. And neither of them Ides is inclined to sit on his backside when he's needed."

"Let's eat a meal off of Brig," said Bill Vainskeep. "I see they got a fair stock of groceries. And we're apt to get tied up pretty soon."

They cooked the meal and ate it. Ute hated to sit there and wait but could see no other course. To him the herd was still the vital factor in the situation. If Loren could scatter it, he had the two-bit ranchers back in his clutches.

Ute sent two men out to relieve Slim and Dory, and when these two had eaten, he suggested that they take turns catching up as far as possible on badly needed sleep. As for himself, he felt too keyed up even to stand still for long. But he needed rest as much as any of them did, and finally he stretched out.

He slept a little in spite of his doubts, and when he awakened it was to find Curly and Slim sprawled under the trees by the creek. He sat up, yawning, and rolled a cigarette. Day had come, and a look at the sun told him that they had not long to wait, for Pick soon would have had time to put in an appearance. Jolted out of his somnolence by that awareness, he prodded Curly awake.

He said, "We'd best get set and do the rest of our waiting where we can fight on the drop of a hat."

"Set where?" Curly said as he raised up and rubbed his knuckles against his eyes.

"We'll take Bill off the south entrance now. We know Pick's bound to come, and we'll see it when it enters the coulee. We'll show Loren I'm the Indian he always claimed and set up an ambush at the east gate where Dory is."

Curly said, "Now, maybe you've got something. If they don't find anybody here, they'll figure we were scared off. They'll try to run the herd out."

"That's right. But we'll turn it back and make them jump us. Then we'll be in the best position to fight. We ought to be able to hold it until help can get here."

"If it gets started," Curly said.

Slim rode off to pick up Bill Vainskeep, who was on watch to the south. The others tightened their latigos and got ready to resume the hard task they had set for themselves. But before Slim got to the southern exit, Bill's horse spilled out of the canyon mouth. A bolt of naked alarm hit Ute. Both sentries had been instructed not to challenge anybody who showed but simply to ride for camp with a warning. Slim whipped around and joined Bill, both streaking it for the camp.

A whole party boiled out of the canyon, then, aware of the fleeing horsemen and rising promptly to the chase.

"Light out!" Ute yelled to his companion.

"It's sure as hell Pick," Curly said. "I recognize some of those cayuses. Lordy, there's at least a dozen of 'em."

Pick's leading riders opened fire but were as yet too far in the distance for effect. The men at the camp sent back a warning volley. Then, as Slim and Bill whipped in, the others sprang to saddle. Presently all four of them were pounding it for the east exit.

Once the others had been swallowed by the rocky jaws of the rimrock, Ute fell back momentarily. Pick had pulled up and was milling about the outlaw camp. Loren, just then, was more interested in the herd than in the escaping men he had probably identified. They were in some kind of consultation at the camp. Ute rode on out of sight into the narrow passage.

The others were waiting for him. He said, "We pegged it right. They're going to get rid of the herd while they've got a chance. Up on the rim, boys — two on one side of the mouth, three on the other. We'll let them get the stuff rounded in and lined out our way. They'll close-herd it, and maybe we can pick off the point riders while we turn the steers back."

Bill took the horses on down the canyon to secure them. The others started up the talus, Curly taking one side and Ute the other. Again Ute had Slim Trawn with him, a puncher he liked to have at his side. The rock, which he soon was climbing, was already hot to the touch, but he had little trouble getting on top the rim. Presently he was bellied down at its sharp edge, looking out over the wasteland oasis.

Now he could recognize the white-stockinged horse that Loren favored and never let anyone else use. They were all at the camp yet, still talking. They had expected to have to make a fight for the herd, were surprised that it had fallen back into their hands so easily, and maybe were a little suspicious. But the opportunity was going to be too much for Loren to resist. Ute was staking everything on that conviction.

The heat of the rock was growing all but unbearable. Ute was soon thirsty, and he wished that there was some kind of shade.

He kept watching Loren's huddled party, and the dotted shapes of the cattle that were spread as far as the distant western wall. Off to his right, Slim had laid out his guns and ammunition. Ute began to grow uneasy from the continuing wait.

Then Slim murmured, "Thank God — they're getting the lead out."

The Pick men were going up to the saddle again. Mounted, the group fanned out. They rode slowly and away from Ute's position. He watched them recede, moving down to the far western end of the flat. They were ready to drift the herd this way.

At last he could see the compacting drag of the herd, far forward. Four riders waited down there, the rest dividing in two, half coming up along either side of the coulee, a man dropping off at fixed driving stations. They threw the steers together, using the ends of their catch ropes as popping whips. Point riders were presently in place, their horses moving slowly.

Ute understood the reason for that careful preparation, which had been the subject of all the talk. They meant to keep the herd under control until they were sure they could scatter it beyond the possibility of recovery.

The cattle, fed, watered and docile, managed easily. They bawled as they always did under march but came on placidly. When they were almost to the portal, the point riders halted their mounts and sat motionless, one on either side and facing the cattle.

Ute nodded to Slim.

They shot directly into the herd, and this signal brought a crackling echo from the three other guns on top the rim. The effect was explosive, the few steers that necessarily had to be hit going down, those about skidding and rearing as they tried to bull back. The point riders simply vanished into a dusty melee. The men on the rim kept up a wicked shooting that soon had the whole herd in a mad gallop to the rear.

"They won't try it again," Slim called, "till they've cleaned us off this rock."

"Till they've tried."

"I sure wish we had some help."

Pick was not long in taking up its unexpected task. Dust still hid them, and the whole coulee was a bedlam of bawling and hoof thunder. But a man cut out of the dust, riding straight at the portal. Somebody on Curly's side picked him off.

Somewhere in the close-by dust a man's voice was bawling: "Get 'em — goddam it, get 'em off that rim!"

"Joe Lake," Slim said. "We're up against

the bigwigs, this trip."

The nearer dust was clearing. Out of its denser background charged half a dozen horses, men hoping to breach the portal and get in behind the ones on top the rim. Yet their intended victims drove them back in hasty disorder. The retort discouraged them, and they scattered, dismounted and lost themselves in the sage.

So far it was going much the way that Ute had hoped. Under siege, they could hold out up here for a long while. He wiped sweat from his brow, watching riderless horses streak outward to disappear where the dust still hung heavily. At least the vanguard of Pick was nailed down by that movement of frightened animals.

It was five minutes, thereafter, before anything else seemed to move. Once Ute saw what he thought was a colored shirt in the gray-green of the sage, and he fired. Whatever it was, it kept still after that. Then a ragged, irregular gunfire opened up on both sides. A slug chipped the rock by Ute's head and he jerked back, swearing. But to fight, he and his men had to show themselves, with Loren's party now better protected by the screening growth on the floor.

But time ran against Loren, even as it was on Ute's side. Sooner or later he would grow restless and try to crowd the decision. The sun kept climbing, growing ever hotter, yet still there was no sign of a rush from below. Then, with full fury, the men on the floor began to fight. There was a volley of carbine fire, which chewed at the lip of the rimrock. It was vicious and meant to drive the men on top back into cover. It kept up a couple of minutes, an up-slanted hail of lead.

Ute understood the purpose of it. In the cover of this attack, men would run forward to get under the overhang of the rim. They meant to close in, hoping to overwhelm their enemies by sheer numerical strength. The shooting broke off as abruptly as it had begun.

Loren had got at least part of his men in under the bulge of the cliff. That made an abrupt change in tactics necessary, Ute realized. The men on the other side of the opening could take care of anything still left in the sage. Ute called, "We got to go down, Slim, or they'll be on us from behind."

Slim pulled back, then shoved to a stand. They started down at once, Ute ahead. He half expected a shot when he dropped onto the talus, but it failed to materialize. They had not yet pressed in, apparently. Sliding and scrambling, he let down to the floor,

Slim close behind.

Once down, they started forward immediately. Ute was in time to catch the first man sneaking into the canyon. He shot even as he yelled to Slim, for he saw a man coming in from the other side. Slim's cracking pistol made answer. Ute's man flung up an arm and, as Ute shot again, spun half around and fell.

Ute kept walking forward, slowly and carefully, Slim across from him and keeping abreast. Another man slipped around the corner, and Ute's eyes glimmered when he saw that it was Brig.

He yelled, "All right, Brig. This time we settle it."

Brig shifted aside even as Ute shot but had come too far to cut back around the corner. Ute was not quick enough, either, and Brig shot from the hip. This time Ute had cut over and again chopped down with his gun. Brig's shot hooked in his shirt, but Brig fell. That was the last of it there. If any others had cut in against the cliff they changed their minds about entering the canyon itself.

Loren and Lake, Ute thought. *Hiding in the sage and sending their hired hands in . . .*

He and Slim slipped on into the rocks at the canyon month. From this floor position they could level a fire into the sagebrush as well as prevent another breaching effort. The firing out there bristled for a time as they realized what had happened to their sally.

The dust from the herd's movements had almost cleared. He could see puffs of powder smoke to fix for him the approximate location of an enemy, but before he had sent forth more seeking lead, he heard a sudden urgent call from out there.

"Somebody's coming in from the basin! Hey, Joe — where are you? Loren — ?"

There was no answer to the outcry. Ute had detected nothing in the farther background but, stretched on the earth, somebody down below had detected the telegraphy of distant impacts. Confirmation came within seconds for horsemen spilled in numbers out of the southern draw. Ute had no better idea of who it was than Pick had, itself.

The shooting from the sagebrush diminished, then came to a full stop. Curly's party also held fire, so that the drumming of horses was a sudden loudness across the space. They were hurried, determined riders, and something about them lifted Ute's spirits.

"One's old man Jorgenson," Curly yelled

from his better view. "That's his dappled gray and no mistake about it."

A shot rang out from the charging horsemen. Pick's horses were in plain evidence, which must have told the newcomers what they needed to know. Pick did not answer, and it dawned on Ute that they were making a frantic effort to escape from between the hammering horsemen and the solid block of the rimrock. Men were scrambling through the sagebrush, bent on survival only, and Loren's foray was already smashed.

The oncomers laced the sage with shooting, while the men at the rimrock lent a hot supporting fire. It was a peaked-up fury intended mainly to rout Pick completely. The effect was quickly apparent. Men began to shove up, lifted arms coming meekly into view, followed by figures suddenly slack and scared. But there were only four of them, which made Ute scowl. Casualties and holdouts could not account for the fall dozen he had estimated at the start of the fight.

Ute yelled a hold fire to his men, then the new arrivals whirled up. They fanned through the sage and picked up the surrendered Pick men. Then all came on to the exit canyon. Ute's eyes held a gleam. Ginny had been busy, he saw. Jorgenson, Windrow,

Ackerman, and half a dozen others were here — every owner in the herd. Told where to make their fight, they had come promptly to make it.

Slim Trawn looked at them and said gustily, "By damn, I never seen a bunch of mad, whiskery galoots that looked more like angels straight out of heaven."

"Where's the sheriff?" Ute eared to Jorgenson.

The old man shook his head.

He mopped up quickly, and the process only deepened Ute's puzzlement. They found three dead men in the canyon, Brig and two more. There were two wounded men out in the sage, where protection had been far better. That was all.

"Loren and Lake were here," Ute said grimly. "We seen them. And they had no chance to clear out when they saw you boys come in. There should have been one or two others from the count we got at the start."

"Bet I know what happened," Curly said. "We heard Joe Lake order Brig to rush the canyon. When they realized it had misfired, him and Loren and maybe a couple of others pulled back."

"Running?" Ute said, shaking his head. He did not believe that either Loren or Lake would do that under present circumstances, when it was a make or break proposition for them.

"No," Curly answered. "To get around and come up in back of us. On foot. Damn the luck. They won't come near the place now."

"I bet that's it," Ute agreed, and he felt the pulling weight of Curly's dejection. He looked at the men about him and said, "Well, we lost the big prize but we made some progress. We're rid of Brig and most of his curly wolves. We've got prisoners the sheriff might get some facts out of. And you boys have got your cattle back into your own hands."

Jorgenson looked at him sourly and said, "We got back our cattle, thanks to you boys. And to my mind the next thing we better do is get them out into the basin. But the prisoners aren't going to do you any good, Ute. Loren's going to claim he was only jumping a rustling outfit when he come in here. It ain't safe for you and your boys to come out of hiding yet."

"That's right," Curly agreed. "The fact that there was a big ruckus in here don't prove a thing as to who was guilty and who innocent."

Ute admitted that, although he hated to do it. He said, "Jorgenson, you boys take the prisoners and get your cattle home. We can at least help you a ways."

"We can handle it," Jorgenson said and held out his hand. "I'm sure grateful. We're ready to fight for you boys, next. Any time you need it, man."

"I reckon fighting's accomplished all it can," Ute said. "I've got to pin the deadwood on the three men behind it all — Loren, Lake and Donner."

"But how?"

"I don't have the slightest idea," Ute acknowledged.

Seventeen

It was in the first hours of that night that Ute rode out of the badlands into the Horseshoe. He had seen the cattle started for home. Curly and his saddlemates were to meet him at Ross Ide's just before daylight. Now Ute was on his way to Pick for a trespass that he knew might prove to be of deadly danger to him.

The grueling night and day that had passed since he had gone into the malpais had resolved matters only to a certain extent. Horseshoe Basin had been removed beyond Loren's covetous grasp. The conflict thus had been reduced to a matter of personalities again — the struggle between the brothers Taplan that had boiled out of a dead man's will.

This thinking had made him remember that marked-up map of Loren's, which first had aroused his suspicions. For that reason he was making this visit to a spread he had renounced. It would either be a quick visit, or he would stay there until the coroner had hauled him off.

This was a desert night, a stir of breeze coming over the sage to bring him a fusion of primitive scents. Star points softly blazed across the heavens and were cheer incarnate above a world made violent by the wills of men. He wondered at this violence and why it was always present. The sky never showed it except when storms gusted across the earth, earth born and earth harassing.

He knew that Loren had stripped Pick of its men, some of whom would never return, yet he began to pay closer heed to his environs once he had topped the last rise and started in upon headquarters. But he was at home here, knowing almost every foot of ground, and he easily kept himself screened from the buildings as he closed in and at last came to a halt. Swinging out of the saddle, he tethered the horse in the concealment of a cottonwood stand. He examined his gun just to make certain that it was ready for quick use.

He came in past one of the big barns so he could have a look at the day corral. There were several horses in the enclosure, which told him nothing of much help. He felt confident that Loren and his companions had been set afoot in the malpais when their plans had gone awry. They had not been seen picking up mounts during the fight, nor had any of the horses belonging to Ute's party been missing afterward. They must have been forced to hike out of the badlands proper, which would have taken several hours. But once in the basin, they could have remounted by taking animals off the range.

Ute was looking for foreign brands now, and he made a long, close study of what the starlight showed him. These were all Pick animals, branded with a T. But that was not conclusive proof of anything at all. He did not lose any of his feeling that being caught here would be to his deadly peril.

After that he moved with the silent patience of an Indian, coming up on the side of the ranch office that was away from the house. That was where he would be forced to risk his neck. He would have to break a window to get in, and he would need light to make his search in the great accumulation of papers he knew he would find in there. He decided to break the glass openly. If the sound failed to arouse anybody, then he could risk a light with less fear.

He took a long look at the bunkhouse, which was dark and silent. He would be detected from there, if from anywhere, for fortunately there was no window in the office wall that was toward the house. He used the butt of his pistol, tapping the upper edge of the lower window pane. The glass cracked on the second try, and a piece of it broke out on the third.

He did not at once prepare to enter. Instead he turned his head and stared through another moment at the bunkhouse. The noise had sounded to him like the crack of pond ice, but he knew that it probably had not penetrated the heavy sleep of whoever was over there. The peaceful wait confirmed that, then he reached in, unlatched the lock and lifted the window sash. Seconds afterward he was inside, hearing only the sounds of his own heavy breath.

He took the blanket off the old couch Tap had used for his naps and hung it across the window. He had nothing with which to cover the glass in the door, but it was frosted and showed itself to none of the occupied ranch structures. His main danger, thereafter, lay in somebody's riding in, in which case detection would be inescapable.

He had a tight tension in the pit of his stomach as he struck a match and lighted the old lamp. Its chimney had long gone uncleaned, and the light given off was not bright. He placed his gun on top the desk where he could reach it handily, then began his search.

He knew that Loren had moved the map the day of Herb Latamore's funeral but felt that there was a fair chance that it had not been taken out of the office. So he went through each drawer of the desk, then through the pile of papers on the back corner of the top. He had no luck at all. He pulled a box out from under the couch and searched it. Yet it contained nothing but old correspondence and records.

He was not immediately discouraged. He had a second place in mind but had hoped to escape having to visit it since it would be twice as dangerous to him. That was the attic of the big house itself. He had remembered on the ride here how Loren had once used a hiding place up there to store his treasures, secretive and unsharing even then. If he had not burned the map, then it might be up there.

He blew out the lamp, resigned and resolved to leave no stone unturned for he felt that, in view of what had been taking place in the Horseshoe, the marked map would be substantial evidence against Loren. He took the blanket from the window, then went out. Unlike the office, whose safe held the ranch's tally books and cash, the house was never locked at night. Getting inside would be easy, but moving thereafter would be another matter. He chose to go in by way of the back door.

Again his intimate knowledge of Pick was a help to him. He and Tap had also slept here, once, but now Loren and Lake were the only ones using the house at all. If they had not got back, then the place was empty. If they had returned, then it was full of possible trouble.

He made his way very quietly through the lower hallway to the foot of the stairs. He paused there, trying to remember just which tread it was that could be so noisy. He started up, pulling in a long breath with each slow lift. Then he was at the top where he turned instantly up the remaining short flight to the attic.

He did not fall to work at once, instead resting and listening closely. He could hear nothing disturbing and felt by then that the chances were good of his having the old place all to himself. He did not need a light to cross to what had been Loren's favorite hiding place in his boyhood.

It was a happenstance of the rough carpentry remaining in the unfinished attic. The roof framing for one of the second floor dormers began at the bottom of the outside wall. That was not in evidence from the attic for, in the interest of insulation, the wall had been finished in unpainted shiplap.

Loren had never needed to hide candy or the oranges he bought in town until Ute came to live on Pick. Afterward he had taken to using the concealed space above the dormer, which he could reach into by lifting a piece of loose flooring. He had never realized that Ute knew all about his secret cache but had disdained raiding it out of pride.

The instant he thrust his own arm into the space, Ute knew that he had what he wanted. The stiffness of the paper he touched told him it was the map. He drew it out with grim satisfaction but struck a match to make sure. It was the map, and now there was a paper clipped to it that had not been there before. Ute stared at it until the match burned out, seeing a piece of Donner's bank letterhead. But it was not a letter Donner had written to Loren.

It was a list of ranch brands, nothing more. Yet the writing was that with which Donner had filled in the papers the day Ute bought the old Arbuckle place. Easy to prove and important to prove, Ute thought in rising excitement. This list was identical with the one he had himself made from the map in an effort to determine its meaning. Donner had given it to Loren, and it tied them together while events had proved much of the list's meaning.

He folded the whole as tightly as he could, then slipped it under his pants band and shirt. At last he had something to hurl at the pair, for every little basiner had examined the list he himself had made from the map and among them they had figured out the purpose. A jury would do likewise.

He was at the top of the main stairway when he pulled up in sudden worry. Horses were coming on, more than one, so close upon the place he would have to hump to get away before they reached the ranchyard. Yet he did not abandon himself to full flight, too painfully aware that danger to him lay also in other quarters. He reached the main floor as the party came into the yard.

He had left his horse where they could not have seen it as they came in. He reached the back porch, which was screened, and decided it was safer to wait there until he knew who this was than to emerge. When the horses passed on toward the corral, he knew pretty well. Someone off Pick was back. It was bound to be Loren, Lake and the one or two men who had escaped from the coulee with them.

He had a hunch then, strong and logical. There was little chance that Loren and Lake had been able to discuss their set-back and plan their next steps in front of their enforced company. He had a feeling that it might be well to wait and see what developed.

It was not long until he saw the four coming back across the yard, all moving as if in deep fatigue. Two turned off toward the bunkhouse, which left Loren and Lake coming on. But they could use the front door of the big house, which was nearer to them. They passed by the office without looking at it, then were cut from his sight.

He knew he was going to slip back inside the house if he heard talking. The front door made its opening and closing sounds. At the back door, which he had opened, he heard Lake say, "I've never been so goddamned pooped in all my life."

A lamp came alight in there. Ute could

see its pale, reflected glow. He knew that they had turned into the front room, and now he began to move, himself. When he could hear Loren speaking, he decided it was far enough. He felt less than comfortable for he was risking his life with nothing to save him but their assumption that he was many miles away.

Loren said, "Pooped or not, Joe, we got to get busy."

"Let me tell you something," Lake returned, "that might not of dawned on you yet. You're whipped. That Injun brother of yours has done it again."

"Shut up, damn you. We still can beat it."

"If you're half as smart as you think," Lake retorted, "you'll quit panting for this basin and set about covering your tracks. I'm telling you, man. You crowd it any farther, and you'll walk into a hang noose."

"We'll pin the rustling on Ute and Curly Jackson. Curly's deserting us sets that up real nice. Does it make sense his leaving a big outfit like this to throw in with that bunch?"

"Maybe it does," Lake said, to Ute's surprise. "Except to you."

"What's got into you, Joe? Scaring out?"

"You bet. The basiners have got their steers back. Even without that, there's the check Donner says the Ide girl deposited for her father with the sheriff witnessing it. That's when I started getting scared, man. Why'd the sheriff do that? Loren, if we were smart we'd drag it before it gets worse."

"And throw up everything?" Loren hooted. "Don't forget I still own half of Pick."

"You bet." Lake's voice turned silky, with a trace of excitement in it. "And maybe it could turn you a real profit even yet. Donner would consider it a forced sale and pay you about what he did Ute. But he'd jump at the chance. Maybe he's hoped for it all along, using you for a tool. Who's done the killing and the other dirty work? Who'd swing if we don't get this thing back on the track? Donner? Not by a damned sight. He ain't stuck his neck out anywhere."

"You're crazy," Loren said hotly, "if you think I'd let him have my part of Pick for what Ute got."

"It would be handy to have some cash if you have to go on the dodge, buck. Don't forget that. But you don't see what I see. Is there any reason you've got to stay in this country where everybody hates your guts and where you're as apt as not to stretch a rope?"

"Joe," Loren said in sudden wonder,

"You've got more on your mind than you're saying."

"Than I've said yet," Lake corrected. "We'll try it your way as long as we've got a show. But the minute we see the jig is up, we're going to Donner. You're going to offer him your interest in Pick and demand cash. Donner will consider cash wise to leave him in the clear. And, son, when that man's got his safe open —"

"Ah," Loren said on a sharp intake of breath.

"You bet," Lake said with satisfaction. "If we've got to quit the country, we'll do it in style, taking the basin's cash assets with us. Letting Donner take the rap where he'd let us."

"If there's no other way," Loren said finally.

Lake's voice lost its blandness then. "Get this straight, kid. If one more thing blows upon us, you'll play ball or I'll know the reason why."

"All right, Joe — all right. Let's hit the hay."

The fact that they would be stirring forced Ute to pull back. But he had heard more than he had expected. It was of no value to him for he could not prove what they had said. It only told him what they would do if

243

things got too dangerous. Lake's proposition made the muscles on Ute's throat draw tight. The man had been in dead earnest. And breaking the bank through robbing it would break the basin, as well.

His only tangible evidence was in the map he had acquired. He had to get it into Breckenridge's hands at once — if he only knew how to locate the sheriff. He crossed the back porch and slipped out into the shadows of the nearby trees thinking of Ginny. She had deposited that check, taking the sheriff along to witness it. Breckenridge's willingness to cooperate was a favorable sign and had worried Lake deeply. Ginny might know where he was.

Ute got back to his horse without trouble, rose instantly to leather, then quietly rode away. Although relieved as to his own immediate safety, a deep uneasiness rode with him. He was leaving behind him desperate, deadly men who time and again had proved their resourcefulness. Loren was not going to accept Lake's plan and clear out as long as a chance remained for him to stay on Pick. Greed for money was only a part of the festering drive in him.

It was not much before daylight when he rode into Ross Ide's headquarters to find that Curly and his friends were already there. Their arrival had got Ginny out of bed, but she looked rested and was dressed and fixing breakfast for them. They must have told her that he was expected for it was Ginny who came to the kitchen door, a hot cake turner in her hand, as Ute rode up to the porch. She dropped the turner, let out a cry and fled toward him.

"Oh, Ute!"

The words, the outcry, said so very much to him, how tensely she had waited, how much she cared for him, her joy in seeing him now. He had no verbal response, only coming down from the saddle to take her into his arms. It was strange to hear her soft crying, to kiss her in this way that was more awed than aggressive.

"I've died times enough," she moaned, "to kill a cat."

"Did Ross give you my message?"

"Yes. Say it again."

"I'll say it better. I love you, Ginny. If I'd been worth two toots on a tin whistle, I'd have known it all along."

"You know it now." Then she stepped back to say, "I'll bet you're starved to death."

"It'll keep."

It kept through another long kiss, then they went into the house. Curly had taken over the cooking, presiding at the smoking

245

hot cake griddle. Slim, Dory and Bill were already at the table, drinking coffee. They grinned for they all knew what Ute was feeling, and were envying him and wishing him the best.

They ate breakfast, Ginny joining them once she had got the men's plates piled high enough. Rolling a cigarette afterward, Ute said, "Well, boys, we're still fugitives, but maybe I did us some good." He pulled forth the map, spread it out, and let them figure things out for themselves. Then, "I just can't decide whether it's strong enough evidence for us to risk turning ourselves in. What do you think?"

"The first question," said Curly, "is where in tunket is that sheriff. Never shows up except to give us trouble."

"You know, Ginny?" Ute asked. "I heard you got hold of him and put that check in the bank."

"I found him in Starbow," Ginny said, "and left him there."

"Time that man was shining his saddle seat a little," Slim said.

"He's no fool, Slim," Ute said. "And he's always been a first-rate sheriff. Didn't he tell you anything at all, Ginny?"

"No. But I don't think he's soldiering on the job. He seemed pretty preoccupied. And he jumped at the chance to help me when I went to the bank."

"Pretty girl," Dory said. "Who wouldn't?"

"Well," said Ute, "do we risk riding into Starbow and giving him this map and Donner's note to Loren — and ourselves, to boot?"

"Must be a safer way than that," Dory said. "Last time we went to Starbow, it backfired."

"Let me take it into him," Ginny said.

"Oh, no." Ute shook his head. "It's getting daylight, and it won't be long till Pick's going to see the window I broke getting into the office. Loren won't have to be told who did it or what I wanted. He'll be worried enough to check the real hiding place. The thing's too hot for you, Ginny, and maybe for us."

"Well," Slim said, "we won't be arrested without the sheriff showing up to do it. If he does, we can make delivery. Let's just wait for him. I'm tired of running and hiding. Right now I'd like a little sleep."

"Best idea," Ute agreed. "You boys hit the hay."

"And you with them," Ginny said. "I can warn you if anybody comes."

"The herd ought to be getting into the basin pretty soon," Ute said. "Thought I'd ride over to where they'll come out. I bought that herd once, but Donner reversed the deal. Thought I'd buy it again if the boys are willing and I can pry my money out of your dad's bank account."

Ginny laughed. "That'll keep. You get some rest."

He grinned at her. "It's your future I'm thinking of. But it's all right if you want to risk starving."

"Rather risk that than having you die on your feet. You scoot."

EIGHTEEN

Ute was up at noon, not altogether rested but too restless to sleep longer. Not so his companions, whose snoring he heard as he arose, brushed the loose hay from himself and left Ide's barn. Ross and Ginny were sitting on the ranch house porch, Ide of necessity and Ginny so that she could hurry to the barn and warn of any disturbing approach to the place.

Ross looked cheerful, better than usual, and said, "Well, the herd got out of the malpais. Tobie Jorgenson was over. Said you were to be here. Wanted to know what to do with the stuff, but Ginny wouldn't let him wake you up. They're holding, now. Just up the country a piece."

"I'll get over there," Ute said.

"And I'll go with you," Ginny added.

"Go ahead," Ide said. "I can hobble around all right today. Anybody shows up, I'll call the boys."

Ute got horses, and presently he and Ginny were riding out. He was worried, all but crushed by the weight of things left undone, yet it was good to be riding with her at his side. It made him think with regret of all the years he had wasted after she had moved into the basin. The years when he had hung around Olivia, not understanding his real feeling for her at all. She now seemed as far behind him as the Paiutes of the Black Rock. She had made her own decision that day in Donner's bank, and was bound to be crushed when the truth came out about Loren. Yet he had no pity for her at all.

The herd had been brought a short distance into the basin and then held. Under the hectic conditions in the badlands hideout, there had been no time to decide its ultimate fate. Ute looked at the massive aggregation of prime cattle and felt a premature pride of possession. He knew that the others would be willing to sell to him, however. He would cut out the he-stuff and market it, but the best of the rest he would keep for breeding purposes.

When he had joined the crew with the herd, he told them what he wanted, and they readily agreed to it. Then, with a dry smile, he said, "Take them on to Rocking A, then. The spread's ready for them, even if the owner has got a little untangling to do to get free of the law."

Jorgenson said, "How about the prisoners?"

Six of them had been taken in the coulee, four Pick hands and the others men out of Brig's owlhoot bunch. "Might as well take them into Starbow and have them locked up," Ute decided. "Even though they'll try to turn the tables on us. And I picked up something at Pick you can take along. Turn the lot over to the town marshal if you can't locate the sheriff."

Ute pulled out the map again and repeated his theory about it. It checked right out with the list he had made, which they had all puzzled over before the railroad drive.

"I'll take Vane and Charlie," old Jorgenson said, "and get going."

"Tell the sheriff, if you see him, that I'll be at Rocking A," Ute said.

Jorgenson and the men he had picked to help him guard the prisoners left at once for Starbow. In view of what had happened to Stub Hines and Vic Rudeen under similar circumstances, Ute felt a little uneasy. But he doubted that Loren would try the same kind of ruthless delivery in the basin, if he happened to stumble onto what was happening.

"Well, they're our steers," Ginny said, looking at the herd with approval. "Let's take them home."

With the help of the remaining basiners, that was soon accomplished. Ute told them to go home, then, themselves. He meant to keep Curly and the others on permanently. When Ginny went home, she could tell them to come on over.

When finally they were alone on Rocking A, it struck Ute that it was the first time they had ever been there together. Ginny wrinkled her nose at the old cabin and said, "It's going to take a heap of humping, but we can make something of it."

"Rather start big?"

"No. I'd rather start right here."

She came into his arms and was not the subdued girl she had been at home in that early morning greeting. His senses leaped at the mounting urgency of her embrace. He said, "You better go home before I lose the tail-hold I got on my baser nature."

She laughed and stepped away, saying, "I wouldn't have said it that way, but I felt something slip, myself. Ute, will you be safe here alone?"

"Don't worry about me."

"I will worry," Ginny said, the elation gone out of her. "Loren will have to be killed to be stopped. You've not done with him, Ute. I'd ought to feel easier, with the herd safe, but I don't. I've got one of those feelings that something dreadful is going to happen."

He did not want to tell her how much the same sense had disturbed him ever since leaving Pick the night before, that he feared this was only a lull in a storm that had not yet shown its full fury. So, laughing lightly, he said, "You've been keyed up so long your nerves are tricking you. But tell Curly and the boys to hustle over here, if it'll make you feel any better."

"I will — and you watch yourself."

"Rather watch you."

Then she rose up to leather and rode out for home.

Fatigue came up in him once he was left alone. He moved into the cabin meaning to make himself some coffee but, when he had lifted the stove lid to lay kindling, he lost interest in that. The vague anxiety that had been in him steadily was strengthening now that he had nothing to occupy his attention. It was a floating kind of disturbance that he could not repress.

That edginess took him outside at once when he heard horses coming in. There were two, and they came urgently, moving down the long sage slope from the direction of Starbow. The sun struck up a winking brightness on the shirt of one of the riders. The other Ute had already identified as old Jorgenson. Baffled, he stood there waiting for them to come on in.

He saw two stern, disturbed faces as the horsemen pulled up before him. He said, "Don't tell me it happened again," in a drawn and weary voice.

Jorgenson shook his head. "Not what you think. The prisoners are still on their way to town. But we met the sheriff coming this way. He had bad news. Real bad. Chance Donner has skipped the country. He cleaned out the bank before he left."

"What's that?" It was not a question in fact but only his mind's refusal to accept the report of his ears. "He skipped out?"

Breckenridge swung from the saddle; he seemed to have had the wind knocked out of him. He said, "That's right. When I just about had him nailed. I want you and Jorgenson to come with me to Pick."

"Last thing I'd expected," Ute breathed.

"You and me, both," said Breckenridge. "I've been in law work quite a while, and I've learned a thing or two. When you've got a situation where a lot of people are divided into two camps and it's plain that one side's lying its head off, there's only one thing to do. Find the weakest link in the chain and hammer the hell out of it. Figured I had it in them two bank clerks of Donner's, and I was right. Fred Tague and old Henry Morse. The day Donner showed us his books with such confidence, I noticed one thing. Morse didn't share that feeling. He was scared sick."

"He's the one that accepted the deposits I made," Ute said. "And gave me the receipts."

"So I found out," Breckenridge said. "But I went to work on Tague first. Seen him on the quiet and told him I figured he hadn't done anything but knew all about it. That he could still clear himself by not withholding that knowledge. Couldn't break him down till you gave me a boost. Ginny Ide showed up with that check to deposit."

"Which is no good in a busted bank," Jorgenson said explosively. "Man, I never had the rug jerked out from under me so fast in all my life."

The sheriff was not without understanding of that concern, but he wanted to get on with the requirements upon himself. He frowned Jorgenson silent. Then, "It showed both clerks, as well as Donner, that there just wouldn't be any mortgages to foreclose right away. It also showed I knew full well what was going on. Tague wasted no time coming to see me. Gave me a signed statement. I locked up Morse."

"Why not Donner?" Ute asked.

"Them two clerks were only the weak links," Breckenridge said. "I don't even know if refusing to put through a bank deposit and lying about it is even a crime. I figured the big links were not only Donner, but Loren and Lake. And it was working. Morse gave me a statement I figured was grounds enough to arrest Donner and scare him into dragging the other two in. There's where Chance Donner skinned out."

"I know Joe Lake was scared almost bad enough to," Ute said, then suddenly he snapped his fingers. "Sheriff, I don't think that Donner really did."

"What's that?"

"I could be wrong," Ute admitted. "But it don't seem to me Donner would skip out that quick, any more than it did to you. Did

255

Jorgenson give you the map I got hold of on Pick?"

Breckenridge nodded. "That's why I come after you. It could be a valuable piece of evidence. I want to question Loren about it, and I'd like you there when I do."

"Well, they almost caught me there," Ute said. "They'd been walloped in the malpais, and that was the first time they'd had alone to talk it over. Lake was shaking in his boots. He told Loren that if things got any hotter, they were going to line out. And take Donner's money with them."

"The basin's money," Jorgenson said on another surge of wrath, "at the same time. As for Donner, I'd say he had it coming. But the rest of us are farther up the crick than we've ever been."

"That's the truth," Ute agreed. "I didn't figure Loren was ready to throw up Pick yet and turn himself into a wanted man. I think I was right. Something's happened to Donner. We better get over there and see what Loren's got to say about it."

He got his horse and the three struck out at once for Pick, Ute now understanding his riding sense of doom. He had feared throughout that the cunning in Loren would show him how to satisfy his ambitions even yet. It was a cunning that approached genius, he realized, yet which required utter ruthlessness to be served.

All but denuded of men, Pick was a deserted-looking place. As they rode into the ranchyard, Ute saw the broken office window he had left behind him. The door of the office stood open. He saw a figure at the desk in there and knew it was Loren.

Breckenridge said quietly, "Let me introduce the subject, boys, in my own way." Then they swung down in front of the little office structure.

Loren had risen and come to the door with a puzzled frown on his face. He looked from the sheriff to Ute, then said, "Well — what's this?"

"Been a bolt out of the blue," Breckenridge said. "Chance Donner's skipped town."

"Donner?" Loren said, blinking his eyes. "What in hell went wrong with him? Take somebody's pretty wife along?"

Ute would have exploded at that except for a quiet look of warning in the sheriff's eyes. Breckenridge was running some kind of a coon, and now that he realized how shrewdly the officer had operated so far, Ute was willing to go along with him.

"Well," Loren added, "come in out of the sun and tell me about it, sheriff. You've kind of taken the wind out of me."

He turned back into the office, the others following. He motioned the visitors into seats, Breckenridge taking a chair while Ute and Jorgenson lowered themselves onto Tap's old sofa couch.

"No woman involved," the sheriff said. "He took the bank money."

Loren had seated himself in Tap's old chair. He came forward then, his eyes wide with shock. "Good God," he breathed. For a moment he only sat there rubbing his nose. He looked like a man who was just beginning to realize what it meant. Finally he said, "This is serious, and excuse my bum joke. You're sure, Sheriff?"

"There was no sign of him in town. And believe me, I looked. I was ready to lock him up."

"Donner?" Loren gasped. "Why?"

"For cause. Henry Morse had a key to the bank. When I couldn't locate Donner, I took Henry over. The safe door was open. Not forced but unlocked. It had been cleaned out. There was nothing but chicken feed left in the bank. Henry said Donner had the only key to the safe. Knowing Donner I think that's true. Bank door hadn't been forced, either. Donner done the unlocking."

"Unless somebody stole his keys," Loren said.

"Then where's Donner?"

"I reckon you're right," Loren said, as if extremely reluctant to admit it. "Why'd you come to see me. Reckon I'm about the biggest loser — but what's Ute and Tobie doing with you?"

"About this," said Breckenridge. The map was bulky, and he had carried it under his shirt. He got it out and tossed it onto Loren's desk. "Recognize that?"

"Sure. It's an old map of Tap's. I haven't seen it in a coon's age. Where'd you find it — at the bank?"

"Ute says he found it in a special hiding place of yours, Loren. And it seems to supply a motive for what's been going on around here."

"Hell's bells, boys!" Loren's fist hit the desk with a thump. "I just thought of something I'd forgotten. Didn't mean a thing to me at the time, but I seen Brig studying this map once. Looked guilty when I caught him at it, but I figured it was just because of him being in here poking around."

"I found that map up in the attic," Ute said. "Where you used to hide stuff from me."

"Brig found the same place, then, and moved the map. Ute, we've been played for fools. Brig had me believing it was you doing the rustling. That two-faced son was working for Donner all along."

"Why'd you have him latch onto me, then?"

"To keep you from skipping the country when we took the sheriff in and showed him that hidden herd of steers. I'm telling you, we'd better bury the hatchet and work together. Pick's in trouble, the same as the rest, if Donner gets away with that money. We got to find which way he headed and stop him. I don't know what you got out of Henry Morse, Sheriff, but it must have scared Donner into skinning out."

"All I got out of Morse," Breckenridge said tiredly, "is that Donner lied to me in a certain investigation I made the other day involving him."

"What you going to do next?" Loren asked.

Rising tiredly, the sheriff said, "I already wired the sheriffs of the surrounding counties. There's no chance of trailing the man. I found the tracks of two different horses behind the bank. They moved onto Main Street and couldn't be followed any farther because of the hodgepodge there. I don't

260

think that means he had an accomplice. He used the extra horse to pack on. According to Henry, there was a lot of silver to be toted. Only thing is, Donner's own saddler is still in the livery, and I can't find where any other horses are missing around town."

"He got special ones and had them handy," Loren offered readily. "Ones you couldn't learn the markings of." He had eased up completely, and it was the sheriff who seemed weighted again by bewilderment and worry.

Had he not agreed to let Breckenridge handle it, Ute would have put Loren on the grill and tried to tear that neat account of things to pieces. So when the sheriff walked out to his horse, Ute followed.

When they had ridden out from Pick headquarters, Ute said, "Well, did he sell you his medicine, Sheriff?"

Breckenridge shook his head. "Not me. But in this work you got to see everything the way a jury would look at it. So far Brig and Donner are the only ones everybody agrees were crooked. It accounts for everything that's happened. Brig's outfit that done the rustling and murdering, with Donner behind it. Standing to foreclose a bunch of mortgages. I could take that, button it up and get some rest."

"You going to?"

"You ought to know better than to ask me that."

NINETEEN

Tobie Jorgenson swung off for home at once, stunned at the bitter way a hard-won victory had been snatched out of the basin's hands. A little later, Ute left the sheriff with only a nod and turned his own horse across country in the direction of Rocking A. Yet when he reached the timber on the dividing ridge, he pulled down and sat there in long thought, feeling the rise of a sudden excitement that had no outward cause.

His eavesdropping had told him that there had been no plan for immediate action between Loren and Lake when they broke off their talk at Pick in the previous night. Yet to reach Starbow, even on a fresh, fast horse, a man would have been obliged to leave the ranch at once.

That was obvious from the requirements upon Loren and Lake after reaching town — requirements he was still certain they had met successfully. Donner had to be approached, persuaded that he was about to gain the rest of Pick at a bargain and induced to go to the bank and open the safe, as Lake had suggested to Loren. Then the treacherous murder, the rifling of the safe, the disposition of the banker's body — and every step of it having to be accomplished before daylight came.

What could have induced Loren to change his mind so abruptly and accept Lake's plan, and why hadn't they then left the country as Lake had wanted?

The fact that two horses had been behind the bank had induced Ute to include Lake in the action. Yet it all made better sense if Lake was left out of consideration. Loren had been the one to suggest that they quit talking and go to bed. His room was where he could have slipped out the window immediately, got a pair of horses and made an undetected departure from Pick. He could have accomplished what had happened in Starbow without Lake's help and with no need to split the profits with him.

He could have gotten out of town, with Donner's body on the spare horse, and also with the money, before daylight came. Yet he still could not have gotten back to Pick in less than two hours more. Somewhere along the way he had been obliged to conceal the man he had killed and the money he had stolen.

He could not have gotten back on Pick

without his absence being realized. Lake and the two punchers who had been in the coulee fight had been exhausted and probably had slept late. Yet the cook and wrangler had been up and stirring at the break of day, according to the habit of a lifetime. They would have observed Loren's arrival. Practiced eyes would have told them that he had all but worn out his horse.

Find the weak link and hammer it, Breckenridge had said a while ago. That weakness now might be Joe Lake. At the first hint that he had been double-crossed, he would be a dangerous, reckless man. He was bound to feel a natural suspicion when he learned what was being assumed about Chance Donner.

This knowledge brought up a sense of driving urgency in Ute. As proprietor of Pick, Loren would remain on the ranch if he possibly could, serene in his confidence that the explanation he had offered for the whole thing would in time have to be accepted.

Lake was not in any such encouraging position. He would try to turn the tables on Loren, and if he came into possession of the bank money, he would clear out of the country. There was no time to wait on the tedious investigations the sheriff still would have to make, Ute knew. He had to take a hand in the rest of it, himself.

Loren was astute enough to know that a showdown between himself and Lake was next to come. Ute swung his horse about and headed back for Pick.

Loren had not yet left the office when Ute rode back into the ranchyard. But he was wary, standing in the doorway by the time Ute rode up. The surprise on his face did not conceal a deeper uneasiness.

"What're you doing back here?" he said.

"Wanted to see Joe Lake and see what he thinks about Donner. Where is Joe?"

"Out with the boys."

"Well, it's getting close to supper time and he'd ought to be in any minute. I'll go over to the cookshack and get me a cup of coffee."

Loren had gathered Ute's purpose in returning but he dared not show that he had. The supper hour would pull Lake and the riders he had left in to headquarters. That would be a critical time Loren must already have been bracing himself to meet for he would have to report the sheriff's visit and why it had been made. His eyes showed their old stormy dislike as they puzzled on Ute. Then he shrugged and walked back into the office.

Ute went over to the kitchen and stepped inside. His entrance brought a look of consternation to the face of old Varley, who had cooked for Pick more years than Ute had lived there. Varley had supper nearly ready, and he swung about with a big stirring spoon in his hands.

"Why, howdy," he said.

"How are you, Varley? Got a cup of coffee to spare?"

"Help yourself," Varley said, with a nod at the big kitchen range.

Just as he was finishing his coffee, Ute heard horses entering the yard. That was what he really wanted. Putting down his cup, he said, "Thanks, Varley," and went out. His pulses quickened when he saw Joe Lake, Jeb Sanders and two others swinging down at the day corral. They looked unperturbed.

Ute turned over toward the office, knowing that was the first place Lake would go after he had taken care of his horse. Loren seemed to expect that, too. He made no comment when Ute walked in. The man's cheeks were stiff, now, his lips ruled. He had a hard test ahead and could not conceal the effects of his dread. Then a shadow was on the window, and Lake came in.

He showed less surprise at Ute's being on

Pick than had Loren and the cook. His eyes narrowed, and a couple of seconds passed before he said, "I'll be damned. The Taplan boys in the same room without tangling. What's up?"

Looking at Ute, Loren said, "Go ahead and tell him. That's what you're waiting for."

Ute was far from as relaxed as he sounded when he said, "It's floored everybody who's heard it so far, Joe, so brace yourself. Chance Donner's disappeared. So has the cash contents of the Starbow bank."

It was then that Lake showed a bald, jolted shock. "Donner — disappeared? Don't give me that horse sweat, man."

"Sheriff was here," Loren said. "I guess it's true, Joe. Had everybody in the basin fooled. As far as Breckenridge knows, Donner just vanished into thin air. But the bank was cleaned out, and anybody can add it up."

"You bet," Lake said with a snarl as he whirled on Loren.

Ute felt a grim relish go through him, for this was what he had banked on. Joe Lake had no roots in the basin, nothing to hold him if it should prove profitable for him to leave. He had been contemplating going as recently as a night back. He was not going to worry about the kind of light he placed himself in now.

Loren was trying to stare him down.

"Well, goddam you," Lake rapped. "When did you do it?"

"Do what?"

"Kill him. Don't try to lie to me, man."

"I'll be damned," Loren said. "I'll answer that with a question of my own, Joe. When would I have got a chance?"

"Told you not to lie to me!" Lake said, a wicked anger boiling in his eyes. "I showed you how to pull your chestnuts out of the fire! And you double-crossed me!"

"Answer my question, Joe. When did I get a chance? We were together till the middle of the night. I had coffee with Jeb and Varley around daylight. Couldn't sleep, so I gave up trying. Before Ute showed up with the sheriff I was still trying to figure out how to nail Ute's hide to the wall. Afterward I was just as busy wondering where I can borrow the money to save this spread. Go over and ask Varley or Jeb, Joe. They'll tell you."

"Bah," Lake snarled. "Them two'd say anything you've told 'em to hold onto their jobs. I've got a better way to get to the bottom of this." Lake had clenched a fist as if to bring it up in a driving punch at Loren. He fooled even Ute in the swift way that, instead, he pulled his gun. He stepped off a pace and held the pistol so that it could cover either man.

Ute's throat was dry and tight but he had been resigned to this. There was only one way to get the truth out of Loren, the way he knew Lake would set about doing it. That was all that counted, for the whole Horseshoe was as good as bankrupt.

Lake was more notably cautious when he reached out and took Ute's gun than when he did the same with Loren's.

"Where do I come in, Joe?" Ute said.

"Dunno what you're doing here. But just you behave yourself. Loren, don't figure one of the other boys'll help you now. They don't like you any better than I do. They're scared of you only when you've got the whip hand. On your feet, now. We're going to the smithy."

"Joe," Loren said in rising concern, "you've got this thing all wrong."

"Shut up. Go on, Ute. I'm not taking my eye off you for a minute."

Loren was a starchless figure as he walked across the yard ahead of Lake but he was still defiant. Ute knew that curious eyes were probably watching from the bunkhouse and cookshack. But Lake had judged the other men shrewdly. Of their two superiors, they seemed to pay the ramrod the greater respect. Nobody put in an appearance.

Loren swung his head to blaze, "You're not going to kill me, Joe — not when you think I know something nobody else does."

When he had stepped into the blacksmith shop behind the other two, Lake said, "Ute, open the vise."

Ute obeyed, feeling cold sweat run down his sides. The blood had drained out of Loren's cheeks, and his mouth had sagged open. But he did not have the courage to defy the gun in Lake's hand or even to meet the man's blazing eyes.

Loren let out a moan when Lake yanked him forward then forced his hand between the heavy jaws of the vise. Lake tightened the vise until the part of the hand that showed turned blood red. He had twisted the hand about until the palm was away from Loren.

Lake said, "All right, Loren. I'm going to count to three, then jerk your legs out from under you. It'll break your hand. If that don't get the truth out of you, we'll see if you can stand the same treatment for the other hand. Cripple you for life, man, even if you can last through it. One — two —" Lake hooked a foot behind Loren's sagging legs and was ready to pull.

Loren looked pleadingly at Ute, read defeat there, and said, "Pack Rat Canyon — I'll take you there."

"That's better," Lake said. "Ute, go saddle a couple of horses. Me and Loren are taking a ride." He loosened the vise.

Belatedly Loren realized that the hold he had held over Lake was gone. Weakly, he said, "Once you've got the money you'll kill me."

"Will I?" Lake said and laughed.

Loren threw himself at the man then, but Lake's gun spat flame. Lake coolly stepped aside and let the driving body fall to the floor.

"Only one horse, Ute," he said.

Ute went to the corral, Lake behind and maybe ready to repeat what had happened in the blacksmith shop. He roped a horse and saddled it, aware of his trembling fingers. Then Lake told him to turn out the other animals and give them a running start. Ute did that, too.

Lake rose to leather, then to Ute's surprise, the ghost of a grin formed on his mouth. He said, "I made you a present of Pick, but I don't figure that makes you owe me anything. Take you a while to start after me, which you will. I'll have to kill you then, which I will. But I can't shoot you down like I did that snake. You're all man." Then Lake was gone at a clatter.

When finally he was able to rise to leather, Ute figured that his man had a half-hour start. He conceded that advantage and was thinking on beyond Pack Rat Canyon. He did not head for it in pursuit, staking everything on his hunch as to what the man would do afterward.

He would go into the malpais, and he could not do it without food and water. While ruthless, he had proved himself a reasonable man so far. He would stop at some ranch to take what supplies he would need to get through the badlands. It was ten to one that the ranch would be Ross Ide's, right next door to the first breaks and the only one so situated. He would have only a girl and a crippled man to deal with there. So that was where Ute headed.

He was barely on his way when he realized that dusk was coming in. But that was neither an advantage nor a handicap to himself or the man he was pitted against. He was cutting across the angle he figured that Lake would ride so did not punish his horse unnecessarily. Thus it took him nearly three hours to reach Ide's, so that he rode in finally on a lamplighted ranchhouse.

He halted before he had come in close enough to be heard by Ginny and Ross for he did not want to expose them to what had to come very soon. He felt certain that Lake, in his calculating rush, would have cut the main road from Ide's short of here for the faster traveling. Now Ute dismounted, left his horse and went down to the road on foot.

He moved so that he reached the trail where three cottonwoods loomed high, and he stepped in under the tree closest to the thoroughfare. Alert in every sense, he began his wait.

He had a grudging respect for Lake, who had never lost his sense of values in the judging of men. He knew that had saved his life at Pick. Lake might have locked them all up there and insured more leisure for himself, but it had been his choice not to hedge his big bet completely. He was no coward, and thus he now became a mortal enemy.

The narrowness by which he had made his interception was soon evident to Ute. On his left, where the road came around a low knoll, there appeared the shapes of a horse and rider. He knew by intuition that it was Lake, not hurrying now and wanting to arouse no premature hostility at Ross

273

Ide's. Ute held his pistol in his grip, while the cords of his neck grew heavy with tension.

The oncoming figure increased in size, past the clumps of bunchgrass and of stunted sage. With each step of the horse, it seemed to Ute that his own shoulders pulled higher. To give himself every chance, he stepped into view while Lake was still on a flat angle to him.

He called, "You never made it, Joe. Hold up."

The horse shied, turning half away, which prevented Lake's driving it forward. Ute hoped that big disadvantage would take the fight out of the man in the saddle. But Lake had carried his pistol in his hand, not meaning to be jumped and taken by surprise. He canted toward Ute, and flame striped the night. Two streaks of it lanced toward each other, and sound split the air.

Ute felt the kick of his gun on his palm and wondered why he had not been thrown back by the bullet Lake had sped. He straightened from his crouch when he saw Lake topple. The man tried to save himself with a blind grab at the saddlehorn. But he fell in dead weight as his horse kicked high and then charged forward.

Not having seen Lake lose his gun, Ute

was cautious and unhurried as he went in. Then he located the pistol, on the ground at Lake's feet. The racket of the escaping horse grew fainter, then Ute could hear the other man breathe noisily. Once Lake tried to bridge up on his shoulders only to fall back with a moan.

In a panting way, he said, "Figured — I'd put you — behind me. You — damned Injun —"

Once more he made an effort to push up. It seemed only a stubborn, spasmodic reflex of will, for with a long sigh, he slumped again and was quiet. Ute bent down, then, to pick up the gun and in that took his fatal misstep. Life surged back into Lake, who brought up his heels and drove his legs outward in a kick-off that hurled Ute back.

The rough ground broke his stride, and he went down hard. He rolled and rose again but was too late.

Lake's ragged voice warned, "Know an Injun stunt, myself, man." He was wounded, lethal as a stricken bobcat, and thus had managed to sit up and reach his gun. It covered Ute now, and that awareness rocked through Ute with the conviction that he was doomed.

Grittily, he said, "All right, Joe. Go ahead and do it."

"Not yet," Lake panted. "I need a horse — and grub. Then I'll do it." Slowly, drunkenly, he climbed to a stand. For an instant he seemed about to collapse again, but will and wrath and the urge to live held him up. Panting, still talking in raveled gusts, he said, "Drop that gun." Then when he was obeyed, "My horse has gone too far for me to risk sending you after it. But I got to have it — and them saddlebags. So we'll go to Ide's, where I can get a better tail-hold on you."

"You'll never make it, Joe. You look hard hit."

"I am hard hit. But you'll give me a hand. I'm keeping this gun in your belly. That's where I'll plug you — if you make me."

Lake must have heard the sigh that Ute could not repress. Stepping in, Ute took the man's left arm across his shoulders. Lake sagged against him but held his other arm across his front. The pressure of the gun muzzle was a looming warning just above Ute's belt. They moved forward, going toward Ide's. The distant windows still showed lamplight, yet the exchange of shots must have been heard up there.

Ute kept his mind on Lake's lurching, sagging steps, seeking his chance to take advantage of that weakness. But the pressure of the metal circle against him never lessened. The thought of hot lead drilling through was an arresting aversion in his spine. Once he thought that Lake was about to give it up. Then new will rose in the desperate man, bringing more strength from somewhere.

When they had come close to the Ide house, Lake said, "Get us in there, Ute — without any trouble."

Ute called assuringly to the house. Then, as they entered the ranchyard, he yelled again, "It's Ute. The shooting's over."

The door was flung open from the inside. Ginny sped through the frame of yellow lamplight. She came running down the steps, then halted to stare in shocked wonder.

"Ute — !"

Before Ute could speak to her, Lake gasped, "I've got a gun on him, Ginny. Quiet, now, and don't you make me use it. Where's Ross?"

"Sitting in the house. Ute — what — ?"

"Never mind," Lake cut in. "And if you put value on this rangy hombre, forget what a wildcat you can be, yourself."

Ute went on, the wounded man stumbling beside him. As they entered the house, Ross Ide straightened in his chair, staring in hard intentness. He gathered the situation silently, and his eyelids narrowed. He did not know all that had happened, nor did Ginny, but this told all they needed to be shocked into razor-sharp alertness.

Lake shoved Ute away with a quick push, sidled awkwardly to a chair and lowered himself to its seat. The side of his shirt was soaked with blood. Yet Ute knew that the life had to run out of the man before the will would quit. Lake swung his gun from Ute to Ide. A kind of grin broke on his pain-twisted face.

He said, "All right. Ute, fetch my horse. Ginny will make me up some grub and a bed roll. If either tries a trick, Ross is going to glory ahead of me." His smoldering eyes confirmed his intention to make good the threat if pressed.

Ginny was tight with rebellion. Again she wore a shirt and levis and was like a spunky boy as she appraised Joe Lake's determination. Whatever had entered her mind subsided. She turned and disappeared through an inner doorway.

Ute swung then and went outdoors. He was caught, and as long as Lake could maintain the tyranny of the gun, he had to obey orders. He walked out to where he had left his own horse and mounted it. Afterward he went to the place of the fight where he found and picked up his pistol. It was useless as yet and would remain so unless there came a chance to use it without danger to the Ides.

Next he rode out until he came upon Lake's mount, which he led back to the house. He tossed his gun into the grass by the doorstep, knowing that he dared not take it in with him as long as Ide sat under the weapon of a wholly unstable man.

He entered to find that Ginny had returned to the living room. Lake seemed to have sunk a little lower in his chair. His cheeks looked paler, while blood had dripped from his clothes to the floor. Each moment that he lived made him an increasingly dangerous enemy.

Lake looked at Ute, nodded toward a blanket roll on the floor, and said, "Thong it to my cantle, then come back here." Ute obeyed. When he had returned, he found that once more Lake had managed to get to his feet.

Ute said, "Joe, if you've got any sense you'll have that wound tended to. You're bleeding bad." The suggestion was crafty, for he yearned to determine how badly the man was hit.

"Never mind the wound," Lake snapped,

understanding instantly. "Help me out, now, and onto that hammerhead."

Once more Ute had to assist him while Lake walked so painfully to the porch and on down the steps. He forced Ute and Ginny to stand back while he made sure the contents of the saddlebags had not been tampered with. Then, with a supreme surge of will, he swung up into the saddle. In that movement his gun was never off the watchers for more than a second. He rested a long moment, then straightened painfully.

"Get on that other horse, Ginny," he said. "You're going to guarantee this Injun don't try to dog me again."

"No, Joe," Ute protested. "I'll leave you alone. You'll never make it, anyhow. Leave her here."

"Never trusted no man yet," Lake said.

Ginny rose to the saddle seat, frightened but showing it only to Ute, who now knew and understood her so well. At Lake's curt order, she rode out of the ranchyard. Lake followed close behind.

As he drew away, the hurt man called, "Don't forget, Ute. She's my guarantee."

Ute said nothing to that. He stood there until the two riders had been swallowed by the night. They were turning north — toward the breaks.

When he went back into the house, Ross said bitterly, "Don't try it, Ute. That snake meant his threat. He won't last long. And Ginny ain't exactly helpless, herself."

"He's stronger than he let on," Ute retorted. "Fooled me once that way. I've got to go after them."

"Can't follow too close. And to ride sign, a man needs daylight."

"Damn it, Ross, you've seen the rotten soul in him. What you think will happen to Ginny, once he's through with her?"

"Go on," Ross said. "That white-face black in the corral is fresh and fast. But the only gun I got's a rifle."

"Mine's just outside."

Within ten minutes Ute was riding out. He was curiously unhurried for, as the agitation died down in him, his Indian sagacity had gone to work. Lake possessed much the same cunning, and Ute was figuring what he would do in the man's place. One thing, he wouldn't want to be hampered by Ginny once he'd got safely away from the ranch. For another, he wouldn't want to be dogged all the way through the badlands, which were problem enough in themselves.

He rode toward the malpais portal, already pretty sure of what he faced. He grew even

281

more certain when his sharp ears picked up the sound of horseback travel ahead. It grew louder, then the night let him see the rider coming on. He spurred his horse and was certain that the oncomer was Ginny. Therefore — Ute accepted what that meant.

As they came together, hauling down their mounts, Ginny cried, "Don't follow him, Ute! That's what he wants. He set me loose so you'd feel free to take out after him. He'll bush up."

"Sure," Ute said, "and I got to have the loan of your shirt and pants."

"My what?"

"He figures to shoot me out of the saddle when I come into the breaks. I don't aim to give him any such target."

She gathered his intentions at once and swung down. She turned her back and, by the time he could follow to the ground, had removed her shirt. Then she stepped out of the levis. She wore only a short chemise but was unabashed in her great need to help him.

They gathered grass with which they stuffed the clothing. Ute forked the legs of the pants in the saddle seat. He placed the stuffed shirt flatwise along the neck of the horse and fastened the rough dummy there. Night would help. From a distance, Lake could not be sure what was on the horse. Not daring to take any chances, he would probably shoot.

Ginny said, "Ute, be careful," and then was in his arms.

She was warm and precious and his forever. He knew that instant of sweetness, then turned. Taking the reins of the horse, he started afoot toward the badlands entrance.

As soon as he was swallowed by the first canyon, his old feral intuition warned him of close danger. He was sure of his figuring, now that Lake and trouble lay just ahead. Ute threw the bridle reins back on the horse's neck. He gave the animal a slap on the rump, sending it on forward. He accompanied it, but over to the right, hidden in the cliff shadow and well screened by rock and brush.

The horse moved steadily forward, giving him no trouble in that respect. Then out of the night and from due ahead came a flash of flame and the sharp report of a gunshot. A lethal anticipation rose in Ute. Lake had taken bait and fired at the dummy rider lying Indianwise along the neck of the horse.

The animal reared, then cut about and was gone at a thumping clatter. Quietly Ute waited, knowing that Lake had been bewildered by that fast retreat for he knew that the man he sought to destroy would never turn tail to danger. Yet Lake was too wary to show himself, although Ute had his position spotted. Quietly, with all the patience wrought by his early life, Ute prowled higher onto the talus across from Lake's station.

He kept well to shelter now and pressed steadily forward. Later he angled back down to the canyon floor, which he crossed to enter upon the far slope. He was then past Lake and certain that the man would be watching in the other direction. He began to close in. He wanted no easy victory. Time and again, in recent hours, he and Lake had pitted wits and courage. So now, with his Paiute stealth, he came nearer and nearer.

At last he saw his man, hunkered behind a boulder and occasionally shifting a little for a quick search of the lower canyon. Lake expected his escaped enemy to come prowling back through the rock and brush and waited, perhaps hungered for that. This was a strange enmity that had pride behind the hatred — the pride of the strong ones in surviving the seeming certainty of death.

Ute passed up the chance to get in the first shot that Lake hoped to get himself. He called, "Looking the wrong way, Joe.

Over here."

Lake spun around. He sent a reckless shot, then threw himself over and fired again. The wild slug whined past Ute's head, the next cut through his shirt at the side. But, between, Ute squeezed trigger and took the buck of the piece on his steady hand.

Waiting in deathly patience, he saw why Lake's last shot had missed. There were no more. The gun sagged down, Lake staring at him in fixed intentness.

"No 'possuming now," Ute taunted. "This time the sand's really running out. You didn't have it, Joe. When you needed it, it just wasn't there."

Lake let out a sudden, raging cry. "You're a devil — !" He staggered forward, but the gun would not come up again. Suddenly he went down and must have been dead before he started, for that will could quit only after the life, itself.

Not trusting him even in what seemed to be death, Ute went in slowly, carefully. He circled and approached the man from the side. In all that, Lake had not stirred. Yet Ute kept clear of the heels that once before had set him back. At last he bent down and took the man's loosened gun into his own hand.

Ginny had not gone on home but had remained just outside the canyon. He heard her relieved outcry as he emerged, then she rode toward him.

Drunkenly, he said, "You're a sight sitting there in your whatchacallits."

"Ute — Ute — thank God!"

Then they started on home together . . .

It was the next morning before they could look to the future. Ross slept on, and when Ginny and Ute had finished breakfast, Ute said, "It's a queer thing. I wound up certain and glad that I don't have Taplan blood in me. Yet everybody says I belong on Pick. I guess it's mine. I'm Loren's heir, and with Donner dead, the other deal can be set aside. Shall we take it, Ginny?"

"We?" she asked.

"If you don't belong there, I don't."

"Then we'll take and build it," she said thoughtfully. "Not outward, the way Loren tried. But upward, the way you would." Her arms drew him tight. Then, in murmuring contentment, "My old Injun. I'm so darned proud of you."

"And you'll be my squaw?"

"Oh, yes. And make'um moccasins and catch'um papoose. Catch'um plenty."